FIGHTING BLIND!

Harrison continued to kick the fallen and now agonized Jesse Howard. He was scarcely aware that he was doing so. The fight had only begun, yet he was breathing as heavily as if he had just run all the way from the Running W. His face was a twisted, blood-engorged mask of raw hate.

A blow, unseen, smashed into the side of Harrison's head, and he went to his knees. He threw himself forward with his hands, curled like talons, clawing for Jesse's throat.

The stitched leather of a boot crashed into Harrison's face. . . .

Leaving Kansas

Frank Roderus

BALLANTINE BOOKS • NEW YORK

For Ben and Winnie Danley

"It is entirely a matter of civilization. The day of the saloon brawl and the painted lady has passed. We are entering a new era in the West, an era of civilized influences. This era will be dominated by men without violence in their hearts. I am a man without violence."

—HARRISON WILKE

CHAPTER 1

Harrison Wilke flicked carefully groomed fingertips across the lapels of his coat to remove any lingering traces of dust before he stepped inside the open doors of the mercantile. His routine upon arriving in town seldom varied. First to the livery to place his horse in the charge of Eli Vandt. Then to John Woolz's barber chair. Finally to the mercantile. His excuse for those visits to the mercantile was a desire to receive his subscription newspapers and periodicals from his post office box. The fact was that Leon Trope's daughter Martha was unquestionably the prettiest girl in town.

This time, though, Wilke tuned aside almost as soon as he was through the doorway and pretended to examine a display of gentlemen's collars and collar buttons. Linen, celluloid and a single fly-specked steel collar with a white enamel surface were all available. The steel collar had been there, unsold, for nearly as long as Wilke could remember.

At the rear of the crowded store, cluttered with a thousand or more items for sale, crammed with tables and shelves, boxes and barrels, was the wrought iron cage that set the postal delivery section off from the rest of the store.

Martha Trope was behind the barred counter now, as Wilke had hoped she would be. She was fresh-faced and dimpled, her blond hair a mass of curls and ringlets, her cheeks full and mouth bowed. She was small and pink-cheeked and given to flirtatious laughter.

Unfortunately she was at the moment rewarding Jesse Howard with the bright, bubbling sound of that laughter.

1

Wilke's eyes narrowed slightly although his bland, neutral expression remained unchanged.

Wilke did not like Jesse Howard. He did not particularly like any of the cowhands he was forced to associate with. Jesse Howard he particularly detested. This was understood throughout the community. The Wilkes and the Howards had been on bad terms for the past dozen years. Privately, Harrison Wilke had specific and clearly remembered incidents he could refer to as a basis for his distaste. One of those fairly recent. He flushed slightly and quickly turned away to pick up and admire a crockery jug of bay rum when Jesse Howard finished his conversation and passed through the store with a handful of letters clutched in his fist.

" 'Bye, Harry,'' the cowboy called cheerfully on his way out. Wilke flushed, angry that Jesse had seen him there. He did not speak.

One of these days, he told himself, he was going to find a way to make Jesse Howard stop using that nickname. No one else, in the family or out, called Harrison by anything but his given name. If Jesse continued, though, there was the danger that others in the community might adopt the habit also. Aside from a distaste for nicknames to begin with, Wilke harbored a sneaking suspicion that Jesse Howard intended in private for the nickname to be "hairy." It was the sort of backhanded joke that would appeal to the rude cowboy because unlike most of his contemporaries, Harrison had no hair on his chest and very little on his cheeks. The thought very nearly made Wilke's cheeks color, but he held a close rein on himself and glared from beneath lowered lids as Jesse went out into the hot glare of the sunshine beyond the door.

"Would you like that bay rum today, Mr. Wilke?"

"Oh. Yes, Miss Trope," he said in a stumbling voice. She had come out from behind the post office cage and was standing beside him. She was smiling but he could not decide if she was smiling at his presence or his discomfort. He found the expression unsettling under the circumstances. "I believe I would." He had had absolutely no intention of taking any of that common scent for his own use. On the other hand, he quickly realized, it would make an acceptable small gift for his uncle, and that would please his aunt if not the old bastard. "I believe I would at that." He smiled back at her.

The girl plucked the small jug from his fingers and carried it with her to the counter, Harrison trailing a pace behind.

"You have quite a lot of mail too, Mr. Wilke," she said over her shoulder. "Did you think to bring a poke along?"

He shook his head then, realizing she could not see the gesture, said, "No." He frowned slightly, but she could not see that either. Harrison disapproved of the use of words like "poke" when one meant sack or container. But then Martha Trope's loveliness and vitality more than made up for any of the minor deficiencies she had been exposed to in these crude, western Kansas surroundings. He sighed.

"No matter," she was saying cheerfully. "I'll find you one." She wrapped the crock of scent in old newspaper and put it in the bottom of a burlap bag, then went into the postal box area and shoveled a stack of tightly rolled newspapers and two magazines into the bag also. There were no letters; there never were.

"And how are you today, Mr. Wilke?" She was smiling as she handed him the sack.

"Very well, thank you, and you?"

"Very well, thank you. Have you heard about the dance Saturday?"

"No." He wondered if there were some special significance to the question. There was a dance in the schoolhouse virtually every Saturday. He knew about them but had never found reason to attend one.

"This one should be special," the girl bubbled on. "The musicians are coming all the way from Trentsville." Trentsville was almost forty miles to the east and had at least three times the population of Redbluff. Locally the larger town had the reputation of being cosmopolitan although Harrison might have disagreed.

"Indeed?"

"They say the fiddler calls himself a violinist." She giggled, as if she found that amusing.

"Perhaps I should come in to hear them in that event." He resisted the temptation to finger the knot in his tie. "Would you save me a dance if I did come?"

Martha Trope dropped her eyes prettily. "I could do that."

"Then I shall be there to claim it." He decided to press his luck. "Do you . . . have an escort?"

"I do."

Harrison nodded, hiding his disappointment. He decided against asking with whom she would be attending. He suspected he already knew. That damned Jesse Howard again. Howard was just the kind of bold-as-brass cowboy who would have asked.

Harrison collected his sack, paid for the unwanted bay rum and excused himself.

"I'll expect to see you there Saturday," the girl reminded him. She need not have bothered. He was most unlikely to let that slip his mind.

When he left the store Harrison had mixed feelings. Delight at the prospect of a dance with Martha Trope so few days away. And disgust with the likes of Jesse Howard.

Someday . . . , he told himself bleakly.

CHAPTER 2

It was barely dusk when Harrison arrived at the dance but already the schoolyard was filled with wagons and buggies and saddle horses tied to the long picket ropes strung between iron posts erected for that purpose. The glow of dozens of bright lamps shone brightly yellow through the open windows, and he could hear the babble of voices from inside. Other people moved on errands of greeting back and forth across the grounds. In spite of his best resolve, Harrison felt a thrill of anticipation.

He walked his horse through the clutter of vehicles and people to the picket lines and tied the animal near a number of others carrying the Running W brand. The Running W hands were already there but Harrison had deliberately lagged behind when they left the ranch ahead of him. He had not wanted the dust of their passage to soil his dark brown suit or carefully laundered shirt with its spanking-new celluloid collar.

At the door he paid his admission and removed his narrow-brimmed hat before stepping into the press of shifting bodies inside.

The men and women, boys and girls in attendance were dressed as well as if they were going to services but there were many more of them here than he would expect to see the next morning in Bernard Cale's small sanctuary. There was not a male over the age of four-teen who lacked a coat and tie, however dusty and stained some of them might have been, and the ladies were all wearing their almost-best. It was a fine spectacle, Harrison thought as he made his way through them, nodding and greeting people as he passed them, being greeted by them in return. The particular face he was looking for here was not apparent.

At the far end of the room a low platform of boxes and planking had been erected with materials obviously kept on hand for just that purpose, but the promised musicians seemed not to have arrived.

"Howdy, Harrison. Haven't seen you at one of these doin's before."

Harrison paused in his search to stand beside the young man who had spoken to him. He had spent most of his school years sharing a desk with Conrad Burton and felt a greater degree of comfort with him than with most of the people of Redbluff, particularly since Con's ambitions were in the bank where he was now a teller. Con affected the rude speech and haphazard ways of his contemporaries, but the past years of close proximity and shared confidences had given Harrison a better opinion of him than that.

"Are you all settled in to the ranchin' life?" Con asked with a grin that said he already knew the answer, he was merely making a joke.

Harrison grunted and made a face. Con laughed. "I thought so."

The few short years that Harrison had been away from Redbluff, living with distant relatives in Kansas City after the death of his mother, had been the highwater mark of his life. To date, in any event. It was only unalterable circumstance that had brought him back. Circumstance that he continued to resent bitterly each time he allowed himself to think about it.

"Your time will come," Con assured him, not unkindly. He lightly squeezed Harrison by the shoulder and gave him a friendly shake. "Don't you be worryin' about it, hear?"

Harrison smiled at him. "I am a realist, Conrad. I don't worry about the things I cannot change."

"That's the ticket, Harrison. Worryin' makes a man old before his time." He bared his teeth in a display of laughter. Neither of them had to worry yet about aging, premature or otherwise; neither of them had yet seen his twenty-fifth birthday. "Listen, you wanta come outside with me where the air ain't so close?'' He gave Harrison a broad wink.

Harrison stood on tiptoe and craned his neck to look around the busy room. There was still no sight of Martha Trope. He settled back down onto his heels. "All right."

He followed Con through the crowd and back into the cooler evening air outdoors. In the few moments Harrison had been inside it had become appreciably darker. After the closeness of twice-breathed air and the odors of sweat and lye soap and toilet waters the night air smelled clean and crisp and very welcome. "Better," Harrison observed.

"You bet," Con answered. His hand slipped inside his coat and came out with a flat, silver flask. "Take a pull on that," he offered. "It'll make your ears turn red an' your nose run, but it ain't real awful once you get past all that." Con did not bother to try to hide the flask from passersby. Etiquette absolutely prohibited any consumption of spirits inside the dance-hall structure, but once beyond the doorway anything was permissible.

Skeptical but unwilling to reject the intentions behind the offer, Harrison accepted the flask and took a shallow sip from it. He smiled. Contrary to Conrad's description of the contents, the brandy was of the highest, smoothest quality. Harrison made an attempt to meet the form of what passed for humor here. "Pretty awful except for the fact that it is free," he said.

"There ya go." Conrad slapped him on the back. "Don't be greedy now." He took the flask back and tilted it. His throat worked twice in a long pull, and he smacked his lips noisily when he was done. "Not too rotten, I'd say.

A group of men idled by, older men well established in the community, and Conrad greeted them with laughing good cheer. He shared his flask with them also and accepted a drink from them when his excellent brandy was quickly gone. Harrison was offered the replacement flask as well, but the sour odor of it told him it was vile stuff. He barely wet his lips with it before passing it back to its owner, and the men drifted away. Conrad seemed quite happy with the exchange. Harrison had always envied Con his easy familiarity with people and his ability to adapt to any company he found himself in.

"C'mon," Conrad said.

"What?"

"C'mon over here. It's a little busy so close to the door." Conrad led the way, and together they ambled away from the schoolhouse turned dance hall. Con stopped at several other groups and accepted drinks from an assortment of bottles and jugs while Harrison patiently waited.

"Listen here," Conrad said when they were some distance from the other strollers. Harrison waited for him to go on.

"One o' these days, Harrison, you're gonna want to get out of here, right?"

Harrison shrugged. "I expect that would be . . . inevitable."

"Yeah, well, I figure it is gonna happen. Sooner or later, if you know what I mean. An' when that time comes, you're gonna want to unload some property more'n likely. When that time comes, well, I want you to think about me, Harrison. You know what I mean?"

"I think so."

"Right, well, a man who's looking to the future, he wants to think in terms of investments. That's me. And a man who's thinking of relocation, he wants to think in terms of capital. That's you. So when that time comes, Harrison, I want you to think about coming to me. It just might be that we'd have something to talk about then. If you know what I mean." Conrad smiled at him.

Harrison felt his admiration for Conrad Burton grow. Only twenty-four and he was already thinking about long-term plans for his future. And it certainly had to be long-term possibilities they were discussing. The only property Harrison Wilke might ever own would be the Running W ranch, which belonged to his uncle. Harrison's father's interest in the property had long since passed to Harrison's uncle. On the other hand, there were no other heirs, so the likelihood was strong that someday, in ten or twenty or forty years, Harrison might find himself in possession of the land the two brothers had once shared. If that were to happen it seemed he already had a buyer for the place. Which would suit Harrison just fine. He smiled.

"I won't forget," he assured Conrad.

"Good." Conrad slapped him on the shoulder with a grin of boyish goodwill. "Right now, though, let's go scout up another snort. Suit you?"

"Suits me," Harrison said amicably. The warm glow of that first drink was fading. He thought he just might enjoy a renewal. He followed Conrad back toward the lights and the people.

CHAPTER 3

Reels and rounds were the normal order of things at the community dances although there were always a few who were willing to endure the slow squawking that passed for a waltz off the uncertain bows of the local musicians. The urbane group imported from Trentsville, though, managed a clearly recognizable version of the waltz, and Harrison found himself once again looking for Martha Trope after the first slow set. He found her by first locating Jesse Howard's bare, tousled head above the rest of the crowd.

"Miss Trope." Ignoring the damnably good-looking cowboy beside her, Harrison gave the girl a half-bow graceful enough to have been correct in Boston.

"Mr. Wilke," she acknowledged.

"May I?"

She gave Jesse a dimpled smile that held no hint of apology in it and laid a gloved hand on the arm Harrison extended to her. "Of course."

Feeling taller and quite proud, Harrison led her onto the dance floor for the start of the next piece. The feel of Martha Trope's waist moving beneath his hand when they danced separated from his touch by only the thin layer of soft material and whatever else she may have been wearing beneath the dress—Harrison did not allow himself to think about that although he wanted to—brought a tantalizing lump into his breast and interfered with his breathing. He was quite out of breath by the time her skirts swirled through the last turn and they stood apart to clap their appreciation of the musicians.

"Thank you." Both spoke the customary phrase at the same time and a moment later burst into laughter at the coincidence. Both started to speak again. Both stopped, waiting for the other to continue.

Martha laughed aloud again. "Really, Harrison, I—" She paused in midsentence as her eyes found something of interest in the crowd toward the front door. She went onto tiptoe to see over her shoulder. Harrison turned to see what had attracted her attention.

Three men had come into the hall, and it was these three who had caught the girl's eye. They were tall, each of them easily as tall as Jesse Howard, and they looked like a rough lot. None of them was wearing a tie and only one wore a suit coat, the other two in vests and shirt sleeves. Most glaring of all, all three wore workaday shirts with attached collars. The one with the coat had a large, drooping mustache; the other two were clean-shaven.

"Who are they?"

Harrison shook his head. "I never saw them before."

"They certainly have their nerve, coming to a dance dressed like they were going on roundup." Martha sniffed. Harrison thought, though, that she sounded more intrigued than indignant.

"I agree." The band leader said something and the musicians jumped into the next piece. Since they were still on the floor, Harrison took Martha's elbow and guided her into a second dance before she could rejoin Jesse Howard. She offered no objection and he counted the opportunity taken as something of a coup.

He certainly was not interested in a group of uncouth newcomers and promptly forgot them under the influence of Martha Trope's sparkling eyes and bright smiles. The dance floor, Harrison thought with no small degree of satisfaction, was a place where he could outshine any rowdy cowboy in the country.

CHAPTER 4

"Would you rather break out that string of geldings then, doddammit?" Stewart Wilke ignored the look of quick rebuke his wife gave him and continued to glare at his nephew. Anger colored his face and he slammed a hard fist onto the tabletop, making a saucerless coffee cup dance and jiggle on the polished wood surface.

"No, sir." Harrison kept his eyes on his plate, unwilling to meet his uncle's look.

"I didn't think so." Harrison could hear the sarcasm in the tone; he did not have to see the expression that went with it. "Hell no, not you. An' don't you be questioning my instructions again, doddammit, or you'll find yourself out *earning* a living."

"He does his best," Nelda Wilke said softly. Her husband continued to ignore her. Harrison was grateful to her although he gave no indication of it.

At the breakfast table his uncle had ordered him out on a days-long sweep to ride bog, looking for cattle mired in the creek bottoms and soggy potholes of the country along the northern part of the range the Running W claimed. Harrison should have known better than to express a desire to remain at the ranch instead, but as so often happens wisdom in the matter had come too late. He had spoken before he had thought.

"Where's my pipe, doddammit?"

"On the stand behind you, right where it always is," his wife said gently. She stood and began clearing the table. This time she did not even bother to give him an accusing glance for his trespass close to the brink of blasphemy.

"All right then." The elder Wilke reached without

having to look where his hand fell and came up with the pipe and pouch of cut-plug tobacco. He filled and tamped the bowl and set it alight with a match drawn from his vest pocket. "All right then," he repeated. It was obvious that he was still angry.

Harrison seldom thought of his uncle without thinking of the man as being angry. Indeed, Stewart usually was angry with the nephew he considered to be a limp-wristed shadow of proper manhood.

In Stewart Wilke's view a man should stand firm, work hard and accept his lot without complaint. He made no secret of the fact that he found Harrison lacking on all counts.

Stewart Wilke himself was a large man, running now to excess poundage around the middle in spite of the hours he spent in the saddle. His scent—he considered it entirely appropriate for a male—was that of dried sweat, old tobacco and yesterday's whiskey. It was unlikely that the bay rum Harrison had given him would ever be used.

Harrison looked through the curtained windows toward the rolling grasslands of the dry, dull country that surrounded them. The pale gray of the predawn was beginning to show shades of yellow and soon the sun would be up. He sighed as he rose from the table and carried his plate and silverware into the kitchen.

His aunt had already put some canned goods and other easily prepared foods into a sack for him. She gave them to him and said, "Have a good time, Harrison."

He grunted. He always found it curious that she would invariably send him off with that or a similar remark, while she always told her husband to "be careful" when he was leaving for an extended period.

Maybe, Harrison thought, the difference was that she already knew that he would conduct himself in a cautious manner. And that it was equally automatic that Stewart Wilke would thoroughly enjoy his excursions beyond the reach of roof and bed. He sighed again. He found life on a cattle operation quite thoroughly awful.

Dutifully, though, he gave his aunt a dry kiss on the cheek, hefted his sack and trudged out toward the shed where the saddles and equipment were kept.

The Running W was essentially a family operation. Extra hands were hired seasonally as the need arose for branding, castrating, cutting and shipping, but for most of the year the ranch was operated by the Wilke family and by a pair of year-round hands who batched in the homestead soddy that once had been the principal house at the ranch headquarters and now served as a bunkhouse of sorts. Neither of them was in evidence now. They would have gotten their work orders from Stewart the night before and by dawn would already have eaten and left for whatever work they had been assigned. Harrison had very little to do with either of them.

He entered the rickety corral and walked up to the most gentle horse in the lot. Most of the saddle horses required a rope for their morning catching, but Harrison preferred those he would not have to fight whenever he tried to saddle them. The cowboys, perversely, seemed to prefer animals that would give them a scrap in the dawn light, which Harrison could neither understand nor agree with.

He caught the horse and led it to the rails, where he saddled and bridled it and tied his groceries at the horn. His bedroll and slicker went behind the cantle, and a pair of ropes were hung at the right of the pommel. Left to his own devices he might have chosen to take a packhorse on a ride that could last a week or more, but he knew that his uncle would scoff at such softness. According to Stewart Wilke, saddle gear alone was enough to carry a man clear across to the Colorado mountains if that was where he wanted to go. Packhorses were for dude parties or serious travel only, to Oregon, say, or down into Mexico.

Harrison pulled his cinches tight and led the docile horse out through the pole gate. "Whoa, boy," he muttered as he cheeked the unmoving chestnut and eased cautiously into the saddle.

"Tsuck." He clucked to the animal and set off at a walk toward the north, away from the clutch of unpainted buildings that made up the Running W headquarters.

CHAPTER 5

High in his belly, just beneath his rib cage, Harrison could feel the cold thrill of a rising fear. It was exactly this sort of thing that made him detest the idea of riding alone to work cattle.

But there was no help for it now. He had to go on with it.

Helplessly he cursed his bad luck. Now in his third day away from the ranch, he was using his second and final rope, and it was much too late to bring along a third or a fourth. The first had broken—been cut actually—the day before when he had faced a similar problem. Now he had no choice.

The damned cow, brindle-colored and slab-sided and remarkably ugly, had been mired in a pothole that must once have been a buffalo wallow. Her calf, also mired, was already dead and trampled in the clinging, clay-based muck of the pothole.

Harrison had made a horn catch on the cow with his second loop and with the help of his horse was able to drag her free of the mud, thankfully without his having to dismount and dig her free.

But now she was out of the pull of the mud and was angry.

Worse, now he could not get the damned rope to flip off of her horns. It was caught somehow and he could not throw it off from the saddle no matter how much slack he gave nor how vigorously he whipped the air with his run of hemp.

By now, in fact, after having been slapped several times with the thrashing rope when Harrison tried to work it free, the cow was wary of the rope and jumped

15

every time he tried to toss it loose. That only served to keep the loop tight around the base of her horns.

Harrison squeezed his eyes shut and tried to get control over his ragged breathing.

If he cut the rope or simply tossed it away from the tie-fast loop on his saddle horn he would have to quit and go back to the ranch with his job only partially done. That would mean facing his uncle with the admission of failure.

Total failure as far as that hard-nosed old imbecile—he was in his fifties at the least—would be concerned. No matter how many bovines were successfully pulled from the bogs, regardless of the fact that Harrison had helped pull a calf from one cow in labor and therefore saved the lives of both of them, regardless of all that, if Harrison came in with his job less than perfectly completed, Stewart Wilke would make Harrison's life a misery for days and weeks to come.

Damn him, Harrison thought. He was not cursing. He was making an actual request.

Still, the fact remained, he and his horse were at one end of a stout hemp rope and that angry cow was at the other. It was up to him to correct that situation.

The fear became even worse as he went over in his mind the steps that would be necessary.

First he would have to throw the cow to the ground by riding his horse around behind the animal and wrapping the rope under its legs to spill it off its feet.

Then Harrison would have to throw the reins to the horse and trust it to keep tension on the rope and the downed cow while he dismounted and ran to the cow.

He would have to hold down the cow's hindquarters to keep it from rising while he used his hands to free the loop and toss it away from the horns.

Then would come the worst part of it. Then he would have to get up, giving the cow her freedom, while he ran for his horse and the safety of the saddle.

An angry cow facing a man afoot is no joking matter. He swallowed hard and looked at the short and thin but wickedly pointed horns trapped within his loop.

Once free, those horns could drive deep into a man's

chest. They could puncture his gut. They could gore a kidney or ram clean through a thigh.

Imagination drew vivid pictures of mortal wounds and endless agony until the relief of death might be granted. The mental pictures were colored in bright shades of red and scarlet. Harrison shuddered.

It might not even be a man's own fault that all of this should happen.

He could do his job perfectly and run with a clear lead on the rising, maddened cow only to have his miserable horse shy away from its rider or blow up in its own fear of a charging cow.

Even the horse might not be at fault. The man's foot could accidentally miss the stirrup. The horse could make a misstep and stumble, so that both of them, man and horse alike, should be exposed to those horns. A rabbit could dart from its hole and startle the horse at the wrong moment. Any of ten thousand things could go wrong, and man or horse might well die because of it.

Harrison tilted his hat back from his forehead and used his forearm to wipe the sweat from his face. The fear closed in on his bowels and he could scarcely breathe within its grip. He wondered, as he often had before, if he was the only one who ever foresaw and worried about the dangers that surrounded this crude life he was forced to live.

Certainly the cowboys seemed never to think about any of it.

They laughed and they drank and they worked at full speed. They never hesitated, no matter what the work or what the danger. They ran their half-broken horses full tilt across ground that was littered with rocks that could turn underfoot at the worst possible moment and with washes and prairie-dog holes that could spill a running animal end over end and break a neck, human or equine either one, without warning.

Yet they never seemed to think about any of these dangers. They never seemed to care that the next rank horse they saddled might throw them and split their skulls against a lump of innocent rock lying nearby or that the next bogged cow they walked up to might break free of the mud in a frenzy of anger and fright and bury a horn in their chest.

Harrison shuddered. Brighter and more sensitive than the rubes who so cheerfully announced themselves to be cowboys, he was unable to keep himself from thinking about such things. Unable to keep those blood-red images from forming in his mind's eye. He wiped the sweat from his face again. The salty fluid was stinging his eyes and making him blink. If he had to go through with this he at least needed to be able to see what he was doing.

He tried one last time to give himself some slack in the rope. He flipped the hemp, hoping desperately that the loop would loosen and he could throw it off the horns without having to remove it by hand. The effort was as futile as all the others had been.

Feeling as if his tongue was lodged in the back of his throat, gagging him, Harrison nudged his horse into motion and turned it to move behind the cow and trip it down onto the ground. A low, keening sound of terror crept past the blockage of his tongue, and he felt a run of icy sweat begin at his armpits and roll down his sides.

It was incongruous, silly really, but the sweat tickled.

He took note of that, but it did not make him feel at all better.

CHAPTER 6

The unexpected sounds behind him were startling, and if he had been a dally roper he would have dropped his coil when he jumped.

"Afternoon, Harrison. Need some help?" He heard the sound of a low chuckle and knew without turning to see that it was Jesse Howard who had come up to him in this predicament. He turned to look anyway.

Howard was slouched comfortably in his saddle, looking completely at ease on a horse's back. It was an ability many of the bred-and-born cowboys seemed to possess, one Harrison acknowledged albeit without envy.

Harrison knew full well that the appropriate response should be for him to refuse Jesse's help. Certainly his uncle would have refused assistance from any Howard or any Howard rider.

Harrison grimaced. "I could indeed," he said.

With a grin Jesse took his rope from beside his horn. A practiced twist of his wrist built a loop. "Get 'er moving just a mite, Harrison."

Harrison nodded. He nudged his horse in the ribs and the animal plodded forward and to the left in response to the rider's guidance.

As soon as the protesting cow's back legs were forced into motion, Jesse's arm swept up and around. The loop of his rope slapped the cow above the hocks and curled around in front of her hind legs. As if it were the most natural thing possible, the cow stepped into the loop just as Jesse pulled his slack taut. Both hind legs were trapped, and the cowboy backed his horse away to pull the cow flat onto the ground with Harrison's rope at her head and his loop stretching her out from behind.

19

"Stay there," Jesse said although Harrison had made no move yet to dismount and recover his rope. He stepped lightly to the ground and his horse kept the tension needed on the rope to prevent the cow from getting up again. The brindle cow seemed resigned to the situation now and was no longer fighting or throwing her head. Jesse called, "Slack," and Harrison sidestepped his mount toward the cow.

"There you go." With Jesse's help the dreaded chore had taken only seconds and there had been no danger.

"Thank you," Harrison said formally.

"No sweat." Jesse mounted in a flowing motion that by all the rules of logic should have required a body without joints or hinges. As soon as he was in the saddle he seemed as much a part of the horse as a centaur. He was still grinning.

Harrison pulled his now free rope in, coiling it as it came to hand. He dropped the finished coil over his horn.

"Aren't you forgetting something?" Jesse asked. He sounded mildly amused. Superior. Harrison felt a flush of resentment reach his cheeks.

"What?"

Jesse jerked a thumb toward the dead calf that lay half buried in the muck where cow and calf had both been mired. "Leave that there an' she'll go after it. Get all bogged again." He shook his head. "Never mind, Harrison, I'll fetch it out."

For the second time Jesse built a quick loop and flipped it casually out. The rope landed neatly over an exposed small, muddy hoof, and he turned his horse to drag the tiny body away from the mud onto solid ground nearby.

Leave it to a man with a bovine mentality to think of such things, Harrison thought unkindly. But he said, "Thank you, Jesse." He did not add any admission that he would not have thought of it himself. Perhaps he would have thought of it, he decided.

Jesse let his loop fall slack and flipped it off the calf's hoof. He coiled his rope and put it aside, then draped a hooked knee across his saddle horn and idly fashioned a cigarette from a bag of makings in his vest pocket. "So what're you doin' out this way, Harrison?"

"The obvious."

"Uh huh. Me too. It's the time o' year for it." He snapped a sulphur tipped match alight and drew on the smoke with obvious satisfaction. "Want some?"

Harrison shook his head.

"It'll be coming dark after bit," Jesse said. "I know a decent spot to camp along Three Button Creek."

The offer was unexpected but in its own way was pleasing. Poor company was better than none after several days alone. "Thank you."

Jesse shrugged.

They rode together in a long curving route that would eventually take them to the creekside after passing the known bogs and mudholes along the way. Jesse set the pace, a rattling jog that covered ground without being hard on a horse although at the expense of the rider. Jesse did not seem to notice the movement of his saddle seat, riding comfortably while Harrison became queasy in his stomach from the constant jostling and jigging. The road jog was the normal gait of the working cowboy, although Harrison preferred to walk his horse when he was alone.

They found one steer that had to be freed, an HH-Connected yearling, which Jesse dragged to solid footing without Harrison's help. By that time the sun was sinking toward the horizon and the afternoon breeze was dying.

"Reckon we could leave that last waller 'til morning," Jesse said.

"If you prefer." Harrison was more than willing to call it quits but he did not want to be the one to say so.

"All right then." Jesse bumped his horse into a lope and Harrison followed, not particularly liking the speed— he always had thoughts about what would happen if he were to fall onto a rock if his mount should stumble— but grateful that at least the ride was smooth at the faster gait.

The spot Jesse led him to was a delight. A stand of cottonwood shaded a bend in the creek, providing wood for the evening fire instead of dried cow chips, and there was a flat of lush, sweet grass nearby. They unsaddled and hobbled the horses, and Jesse began gathering wood while Harrison assembled the makings for a meal. By the time it was fully dark they had finished their meal and had a second pot of coffee boiling on the coals.

"Not entirely rotten," Jesse observed as he rolled another smoke.

Harrison disagreed—he did not care for camp fare—but he did not make an issue of it. He grunted something that could have been taken to mean assent and wrapped his hands around the lingering warmth in his crockery—he detested tinware—coffee cup. The nights seemed always chill no matter the heat of the days here.

Jesse lighted his cigarette and pulled his saddlebags closer. Incredibly, he pulled a large revolver from the right-hand bag and brought out a cloth to wipe the weapon with.

"Whatever are you carrying that thing for?" Harrison asked. No one carried firearms anymore, not around Redbluff, not since the now gone days of the old-time trail drovers, although Harrison had heard that some men carried rifles over in Colorado, where there was still a problem with predators. But a revolver? That was the stuff of lurid dime novels published in New York by people who should have been sensible enough to know that what they had there was infinitely more desirable than any imagined romance of the dusty plains. Harrison frowned. The realities of the cattle business were long hours, filth, danger and few baths. And it was most unusual that anyone he personally knew might be carrying a weapon. Most unusual indeed.

Jesse had the revolver partially disassembled and was carefully wiping it inside and out. He looked up and asked, "Do you mean you haven't heard?"

CHAPTER 7

"Some son of a bitch has taken to stealing livestock."

"What?"

"Stealing stock. You know, rustling."

"I understood what you said, I simply . . . find it difficult to believe."

"Yeah, I know what you mean." A clot of gray ash fell from the tip of Jesse's cigarette as his lips moved. The ash dribbled down the front of his vest. He either did not see it fall or chose to ignore it.

"Nothing like that has happened since . . . I cannot remember when it might have been."

"Not since the last of the Indians was run off is the way my daddy recalls it. You and me was pretty little back then."

Harrison motioned toward the revolver, which Jesse was in the process of reloading with five stubby, brass cartridges. "Are you competent with that?"

"I reckon." Jesse grinned. "Makin' you nervous, am I?"

"As a matter of fact, you are."

"I'll put it away then." He shoved the weapon back into the saddlebag pocket and put the flap over it. Harrison noticed, though, that he did not buckle the flap shut.

"Tell me more about the, uh, theft."

Jesse shrugged. More ash dribbled down his chest and belly into his lap. This time he brushed it away. "Not much to tell at this point. It was some of our stuff that was stole. Twenty steers or so, coming two-year-olds. Whoever took 'em picked them up out of a grass swale on the north end of the place and drove them east.

Didn't leave much in the way of tracks. Not enough to follow far though we sure as hell did try. Daddy went over to Trentsville to file a complaint an' see if they was sold over there, but he don't figure it will do no good.''

"With any luck it was an isolated happenstance caused by some passer-through." Harrison shook his head. "There are such ruffians drifting about these days."

"Yeah, well, we've had it pretty lucky for a long time. Gotten kinda used to things being soft. If those times are changing we'll just do what we have to do, that's all. Do what we have to do." He patted the saddlebag flap that lay over the big revolver, and Harrison felt a chill that had nothing to do with the soft, cool evening air.

"I doubt it will come to that," he said hopefully.

"Whatever." Jesse Howard sounded as if he did not much care whether the future held violent trouble or not.

"Ours is a civilized society," Harrison protested. "We cannot condone anything less than civilized behavior."

Jesse grinned at him again, an indulgent expression such as a mature adult might give to a child. "Ain't you heard, Harry? It takes two to make a bargain. But only one to make a fight. Any son of a bitch that wants to steal from the HH-Connected, well, he's made himself a fight."

Harrison shuddered. He had no doubt that Stewart Wilke would react precisely the same way. That was a barbaric outlook to Harrison's way of thinking but it was what he should expect from the unbathed rustics who populated this unprepossessing land.

Jesse removed his boots and then his hat and rolled into his blankets without bothering to brush himself free of the grasses and bits of dirt that clung to the seat of his trousers. That, Harrison thought, was a significant indicator of the differences between the two young men. He brushed and folded each article of clothing as he disrobed in preparation for going to bed.

It was some time before Harrison's breathing fell into the slow, shallow patterns of sleep.

CHAPTER 8

"Doddammit, boy, didn't you hear me? Thirteen head of Running W stock carried off who knows where and come morning you figure to go to *town?*"

"Tomorrow is the Sabbath," Nelda Wilke said softly.

"I *know* that. So do those damn thieves know it. The only reason I come in at all tonight is to get me some men an' some guns before I taken off after them. Jesus!"

"You will mind your manners at table, Stewart Wilke."

"I'll also be twenty mile east of here come daybreak, doddammit. Now are you riding with me or not, boy?"

"You know I would be of no assistance," Harrison said calmly.

"By God, boy, that's the truest thing I've heard you say in a helluva long while. By God, it's so."

"*Stewart!*"

"Shut up, old woman, I got no mind to be polite tonight."

"That, sir, is obvious."

"If you don't want to listen, go somewheres else, woman." He ignored her while his wife gathered her skirts and her plate and hurried out of the room. Harrison prudently kept his eyes on his own plate.

"No, by God, that's the truest thing you've said in a while, boy. Well all right. I don't know how long me and the boys will be gone. You stay here an' do the choring." He grunted. "I'd tell you to strap a gun on like the rest of us except you prob'ly wouldn't know what to do with it anyhow."

"No, sir, I probably would not." Harrison could dimly recall an abortive attempt by his father to teach him to shoot. It was one of the few memories Harrison had of his father; he must have been not more than seven or eight at the time. The primary thing he remembered about that moment now was his father's anger at Harrison's ineptitude. He had been unable to keep either eye open when he knew a loud noise and a walloping shock was about to happen. As far as he could recall he had not touched a firearm of any kind since that time.

Stewart bolted the food on his plate without taking time to taste it. Harrison doubted that he even knew what it was. As soon as he was done he shoved the plate aside and stalked into his "study," the dark room of leather and antlered heads and aged whiskey where Stewart preferred to spend his few indoor moments. Not knowing what else to do with himself, Harrison followed.

"You make damn sure the saddle stock's fed and watered, boy, and do the house chores an' such. At least that way you'll be doing *some*thing useful. And if you just haveta go into town tomorrow you can find Luther MacRae and tell him what's gone on out here."

"Mr. MacRae is only the town constable. Shouldn't you report this to the county sheriff?"

"If you'll let me *finish*," Stewart said with a glare, "you should tell Luther to make the report over to Trentsville. I ain't gonna waste my time goin' over there for nothing."

"Yessir."

Stewart was rummaging in a lower drawer of his desk, removing pasteboard boxes of cartridges and stacking them on the paper-littered desk surface. From another drawer he pulled out a holstered revolver and laid it with the ammunition. Harrison got the impression there must have been enough ammunition there to conduct a brisk skirmish if not an entire war. If he had ever seen the revolver before he could not remember it although he was not particularly surprised that his uncle owned one. Stewart and Harrison's father had been trail drovers in their youth, and Harrison would have been able to believe very nearly anything about the two of them in those days.

"Hand me that Winchester, boy. The '73 model."

Harrison inspected the rack of rifles and shotguns on

the wall. He was sure of the difference between those two categories but any further differentiation was beyond him. He got down one of the rifles at random.

"No, doddammit, I said the '73 model. The .44-40 one on the top there."

"Right." Harrison replaced the rifle he had taken down and got down the one his uncle wanted. As far as he could determine there was no visible difference between the two.

"That's better. An' I need the saddle scabbard from that chest over there. Bottom drawer. There's field glasses in there too; fetch them out. Anything else?" Stewart was obviously talking to himself when he asked the question. It was unlikely he would have solicited Harrison's opinion. "No, I reckon not," he answered himself. "That should do it."

"Do you want me to ask Aunt Nelda to fix you a sack of food?"

Stewart shook his head. "No need. We're traveling light an' fast. We'll kill some meat as we need." He reconsidered. "Maybe a poke of ground coffee. Though it makes me think I'm gettin' old and soft wanting coffee on a run like this'uns gonna be."

Old, Harrison could agree with. Soft, no. He went to tell his aunt.

Minutes later Stewart and the two hands were gone, swallowed quickly by the darkness. Wilke could find the place where he had last seen the thieves' tracks in the dark. He intended to be there by first light.

Harrison shook his head. In good conscience he could not wish his uncle well. A few head of free-breeding cattle could hardly be considered worth a man's life.

CHAPTER 9

". . . Amen." As one, the congregation raised their heads and Bernard Cale joyously lifted his arms to bring them to their feet. "Join me now in singing our closing hymn, 'The Old Rugged Cross.' "

The piano picked up the tune, and the voices, vigorous if untrained, swept into the song. There were no hymnals. None were needed.

Harrison sang with them, hardly conscious of the words that came from his mouth. His eyes cut sideways toward Martha Trope on the opposite side of the church. Between them were perhaps a dozen people, all dressed in their best, and the polished wooden pews that two years ago had replaced the stark, uncomfortable benches that used to be in the sanctuary. Harrison caught Martha's eyes swinging his way and felt a flush of pleasure. He smiled at her.

Minutes later, the service concluded, he hung back and let the others file out ahead of him to shake hands with Bernard—Pastor Cale only to strangers, Bernard to nearly all of the community—and wander toward the grove of trees where picnic lunches were laid out on the tall benches provided for that purpose. Most of the men pulled pipes or plugs of chewing tobacco from their pockets as they exited the church. The women broke into birdlike chatter as they walked arm in arm with their husbands, smiling and waving and calling gaily from one pair to another.

"That was a fine sermon this morning, Bernard," Harrison said when it came his turn to shake Cale's hand and present his Sunday smile. "Excellent."

"Thank you, Harrison," Bernard clapped him affectionately on the shoulder and gave him a friendly shake. "See you outside?"

"Of course." The routine seldom varied. Harrison had his lunch more or less alone while the preacher met his social obligations by moving from group to group and family to family, then Harrison and Cale walked to Cale's rented house for a game of chess.

"Thank goodness for clement weather," Cale had said on more than one occasion. "Lawn lunches get me out of those endless chicken dinners and those parades of unmarried daughters and cousins and spinster kinfolk." He always smiled when he said it but there seemed to be more than a grain of truth expressed.

A bachelor by choice, Bernard Cale was in his late twenties but looked much younger. He had come to Redbluff as a last resort, both for himself and for the community in search of a pastor, fresh from seminary and looking like a teen-age pretender to the holy calling, but he had grown to be a part of the community, if from a slight distance. Most of the people had come to accept him as well intentioned and genuine even if they did not know him well. More important, time had given them a sense that he was theirs. It was an acceptance of sorts.

Harrison left the church and joined the slow-moving stream of churchgoers strolling toward the tables. Most of them were townspeople but there were a handful of families in from the closer ranches as well. The ranch families were represented for the most part by wives and children while the men stayed at home.

Around the tables the groupings shifted, families separating into knots of men here, smaller knots of women-folk there and children milling through and among them all. Harrison found Luther MacRae and reported his uncle's troubles.

The constable, who was primarily the town blacksmith and only doubled part-time as a peace officer, frowned. "That's the second theft report I've heard in a week. Not the usual sort of thing around here. Don't know what I can do about it though."

"He just wants you to make a report over to the county seat, Mr. MacRae."

"I can do that right enough," he said with a nod. He was a serious man, given to consideration before action. Frequently he was given to consideration instead of action. "Tomorrow. I can put a report in the mail tomorrow."

"Is there any likelihood a deputy could be sent here to investigate?" Harrison asked.

"Mmm. I wouldn't know about that. Not up to me, you know."

"I know that." Harrison also knew that the possibility was slight at best. Redbluff was seldom visited by county officials even at election times; the voting bloc in and around Trentsville was so much larger than Redbluff's that the latter's opinions and problems were seldom considered.

"Make sure your uncle knows that, Harrison. It isn't up to me."

"Yes, sir," Harrison said dutifully. Stewart Wilke already knew he could expect no official help. That was part of the problem as far as Harrison was concerned. He turned away and went to locate the basket of food-stuffs he had brought.

"In a hurry, Harrison?"

"What? Oh, it's you." A smiling Bernard Cale had hold of his elbow.

The smile became broader. "Were you expecting Miss Trope perhaps?"

Harrison blushed. "Of course not."

"I couldn't help noticing from the pulpit this morning where your attention was." Bernard patted him on the shoulder. "As it happens, the Tropes have asked me to take my lunch with them. Why don't you join me?"

"They wouldn't—"

"They wouldn't mind a bit." Cale pulled him along by the coat sleeve. Harrison's protests were only tokens.

"Folks," he said when they reached the bench, "I'd been planning to eat with Harrison here. You wouldn't mind if he joined us, would you?"

Harrison was remotely aware of the elder Tropes' acceptance of the suggestion. He was much more aware of Martha's brief smile and lowered eyes.

This promised to be a fine afternoon, he decided.

CHAPTER 10

Harrison selected a flat, speckled pebble and flipped it. The stone skipped once before landing with a soft plop and settling to the bottom of the clear pool below the bend of the stream.

"It's so quiet," Martha mused. She was sitting on the moist, bankside grass in the shade of a cottonwood. The spot was only a few hundred yards from the church building but it had a feeling of remoteness. "During the week there is always some kind of noise. Wagons moving and people talking and Mr. MacRae pounding on his anvil." She sighed and drew her knees up, wrapping her arms around them and smoothing the skirt of her dress down so that nothing improper would be displayed. "I do enjoy Sundays."

Harrison cleared his throat but could think of nothing to say. He tried to skip another pebble but managed only to plunk the stone into the water.

"Are you sure you don't mind missing your game?"

He shook his head.

"You're very shy, aren't you?"

Harrison picked up another pebble and examined it closely. "I suppose," he mumbled.

"You needn't be," the girl said.

Harrison could feel his face grow warm. He turned his head away from her and threw the pebble. He had not been trying to skip it this time and, perversely, the pebble skittered perfectly across the pool surface, touching at least four times before it finally lost momentum and sank.

"Do I make you nervous, Mr. Wilke?"

"Somewhat." He expected her to laugh in response

31

to that admission and he turned quickly to catch her at it but instead the girl's expression was serious.

"I don't intend to," she said.

Harrison looked away from her again. "I am sure you do not," he said stiffly.

"Tell me about yourself."

He said nothing.

"All right. I'll tell you. You are very shy, Mr. Wilke, and very intelligent. You are sensitive. I think you feel out of place here. That you could open up and reach your full potential elsewhere but not here. Am I correct so far?"

He shrugged but refused to look at her again.

"I believe I am. I . . ." She hesitated, as if she was trying to decide if she should go any further. Softly she continued. "My father told me something once that helps me whenever I begin to feel discontented." She stopped again, obviously expecting an invitation to continue, but Harrison was silent.

"He told me," she said, "that opportunity, like success, comes from people, not from places."

He turned his head to look at her but the mockery he had feared he might see in her eyes was not there. She looked guileless and sincere. And very pretty.

"I've thought about that quite often," she said. "I believe he may have been right." She smiled. "But I hadn't intended to become so serious. After all, we are enjoying a lovely Sabbath afternoon. Help me up, Mr. Wilke, and we can walk back to join the others. It sounds like someone has started some games."

She held her hands out and Harrison had no choice but to go to her and help her to her feet. In the direction of the church grove they could hear voices shouting and cheering, which probably meant that someone had organized the children into footraces or a ball game or some such contest.

Harrison accompanied the girl up the slight rise away from the stream and back toward the company of the others.

CHAPTER 11

Someone had produced a tattered semblance of a base-ball, and someone else had found a length of wood that approximated a bat. The bases they had laid out were scuffed areas on the ground that gave Bernard Cale, acting as umpire, plenty of leeway in determining who was or was not safely on base at any given moment. Even the men had taken their coats off and were in their shirt sleeves acting as teammates for their sons while the daughters looked on with alternate shrieks of agony or delight, depending on what the manly players were doing.

Harrison had no intention of joining them but no sooner were he and Martha in view than Bernard was calling for him to take the field with Tom Trope, John Byers and a flock of half-sized but highly enthusiastic small boys. Harrison tried to refuse, but by then Bernard and Trope had him by the elbows and were propelling him bodily onto the field.

Martha, he saw, laughed her way to the sidelines to join her mother and a group of women standing there in support of their stalwarts.

"Play ball!" Bernard called.

Harrison had little idea what was expected of him, so he stood where he was and waited for either inspiration or understanding.

The pitcher was twelve-year-old Larry Ricks. The youngster went into an arm-whirling windup and spat out of the corner of his mouth the way he had seen his elders do when the town ball team opposed players from other communities. He let fly with a sharp cast of arm and wrist, and the ball sailed in the general direction of the batter.

33

Tim Bartlett, older but not apparently wiser than his opponent, took a vigorous but poorly aimed swing at a pitch that crossed the plate slightly above the height of his head, and the catcher leaped high in the air to snag the thing before he would have to chase after it.

"Strike three," Bernard called. "You're out."

Tim kicked once at the folded rag that was serving as home plate and handed the bat to the next would-be hitter.

The others in the field were clapping their hands to applaud the talents of their pitcher, so Harrison joined them. Not an entirely unpleasant sport, he decided. When the others yipped and yelled and cat-called at the batter he joined them in that too and felt actually quite pleased about the whole thing.

"Come on now. Yo, team, yo," he yelled.

One more out, gained on a pop-up fly into the cap of Larry's ten-year-old brother Louis, and Harrison's team trotted in for their turn at bat.

"Now we have them, team," Harrison yelled. He had no idea what the scores were, if any, and he did not particularly care.

Larry was their first batter. He watched two balls and on the third pitch ticked the ball into a bouncing dribbler that squirted between the enemy's basemen and eluded their outfield long enough for the grinning youngster to reach the general area designated as second base.

"That's the way, Larry. That's the boy." Harrison was clapping his hands.

"You're up, Harrison."

"What?"

Martha's father, who seemed to be in charge of the team as much as anyone, gave him a shove toward the plate. "You haven't had a chance at bat yet. Go on."

The enthusiasm drained swiftly away and Harrison felt a chill at the idea of all those people watching him make a fool of himself.

"Go on, Harrison."

"I don't know how."

Trope laughed. "You can't do any worse than I did.

Been up twice and struck out both times. Hurry up."
He gave Harrison another nudge toward the plate.

Reluctantly Harrison accepted the bat that was handed
to him. He had seen the game played often enough
before but had never attempted it himself. It might have
been different had they played it when he was in school,
but the rage of baseball had occurred too recently for
that.

"Just hit the ball and run like mad," Trope said. "If
you miss, don't worry about it. We're going to whup 'em
bad."

Harrison grinned and shrugged. It was only a game,
after all. "All right."

He took his stance the way he had watched others do
it and waggled the end of the stick that was their bat. He
took a practice cut through the air. The bat felt awkward
in his hands but it swished through the air with authority.

For a brief moment he had a clear vision of himself as
a hero of the town. J. J. York, fourteen years old and
trying very hard to have people call him a mature and
dignified Jay instead of the childish JayJay, was the
opposing pitcher.

JayJay would throw that old ball and Harrison would
hit it hard and clean and far. The thing would arc high
into the air and come to earth, why, practically in the
next county.

It would be a home run. The winning run. They would
all be cheering and shouting and calling his name as he
trotted in triumph around the bases. Harrison could
practically feel it happening.

He waggled the end of the bat again. "Throw it in
here, JayJay," he called. No, that was not right. And he
was feeling magnanimous. "Pitch it to me, Jay." That
was better. He wanted to give the kid *some* satisfaction,
and the older-sounding name was much nicer.

JayJay went into a windup at least as lengthy and
easily twice as intricate as Larry's had been. He reared
back and whipped his arm forward.

'Strike."

Harrison had been ready, or so he thought, but he had
not had time to get the bat off his shoulder before the

ball was already past. Darn, he told himself. Their catcher tossed the ball back to his pitcher.

"One more time," Harrison called if with a little less enthusiasm this time.

JayJay went into his windup, and this time Harrison set himself for the swing. The ball left JayJay's hand and Harrison took a vicious swipe at it. He was nearly turned around by the time the ball reached the catcher, but his swing had at least come close to the pitch. He was sure of that. And he was determined. He scowled.

"You're doing fine," he heard someone call to him. "You're still alive, Harrison. Good swing. Good cut, boy."

JayJay caught the returned ball and grinned at Harrison. Harrison grunted. Timing, that was the thing.

"Watch it come to you, Harrison. Keep your eye on the ol' ball there."

One more strike and he would be out. He turned to see who was talking to him. It was Tom Trope. At least no one seemed to be upset with him so far. He turned back just in time to see JayJay's arm whip forward.

Damn, he muttered to himself. He had no time to get set.

In desperation he lashed out across the plate, not really aiming at the thrown ball but reacting to the fact that it had been thrown.

Amazingly, satisfyingly, he could feel a sudden, tingling shock in his hands and heard the crack of wood on stretched hide.

The ball flew up and out, and Harrison stood watching its travel.

"Run, Harrison. Run for the base."

Someone grabbed the bat from his hands and gave him a push down the baseline. Belatedly he realized what he was supposed to do. He started to run.

He pounded down to first and turned the corner, arms pumping and excitement growing in his chest. He had no idea where the ball was, but he was sure that he must have hit a home run. He must have.

He reached second and turned for third. He could hear the yelling now. Bert Grant was their third baseman.

Bert was shouting toward his outfielders and trying to hurry them with contortions of his lanky frame. He was clapping and shouting and dropping to his knees to reach for something. On the sidelines everyone else was shouting and jumping too. Harrison ran across the area that was the third base and began a heart-pounding gallop for home plate.

The catcher was standing in his path, waving his arms and shouting. Harrison charged straight for him, straight for the glory of a home run.

He felt something jar his side.

"You're out," Bernard called.

"What?" Harrison came to a halt with his lungs burning and his chest heaving. "What happened?"

Trope and the rest of his team were grinning and pounding him on the back. "Great hit, Harrison. Great run.

"Did I hit a home run?"

"No, they threw you out. But it sure was fine."

Harrison bent over, gulping for oxygen, feeling a sharp pain in his side. "Da—drat."

"No, it's fine, Harrison. You drove Larry in for us. You did good, boy."

Harrison looked around. Larry Ricks was being congratulated for scoring Harrison's run.

Still, the men and the boys were congratulating Harrison too. They were all in high spirits. And he had been the one to make that hit. It had not been a home run. But he had caused the score to be made.

He grinned and tried to work some spittle into his dry mouth. The stitch in his side was still there, but he did not mind it greatly.

Feeling magnanimous—again if not still—Harrison limped over to the small boy who had crossed the plate safely and offered his congratulations too. "Good going, Larry."

Harrison felt rather good himself, actually. He turned and began to clap his encouragement of his team's next batter.

CHAPTER 12

"Do you think Uncle Stewart will be back tonight?"

Nelda shrugged and poured the last of the coffee into their cups. Lingering at the table was not done when Stewart was around, but Nelda did not seem to mind it. Certainly Harrison did not.

"He will stay out as long as it takes," she said. She got a faraway look in her eyes. "I remember, oh, it must be twenty-five years ago or more. Before you were born anyway, before your daddy married, Stewart and your dad were just trying to get this ranch started. Some men passing through on their way to the gold fields in Colorado tried to steal a supply of beef. I guess they wanted to sell or trade them when they reached the mountains. We understood that beef was scarce there and the game nearly all gone. In any event, they took some of our cattle, and we had precious little to spare back then. Just a sod house that the three of us shared and a few stock cows. Those and a great deal of hope." She stirred sugar into her cup without seeming to be aware that she was doing it.

"There were still Indians to worry about then. The Southern Cheyenne, who weren't really all that bad, and sometimes some Kiowa, who were worse than bad. It was early in the season with the grass newly greened and the Indians moving. Some of the cows were still calving. It was no time of year for the men to be gone, and of course we had no hired hands back then. Couldn't afford wages. We were just getting by.

"Your daddy came in one day, though, and said we had lost some stock. He found the tracks. Days old by then. The wise thing to do probably would have been for

38

Stewart and your dad to accept the loss and keep on here, but I don't believe either one of them ever considered that.

"They left me here with a pistol and two shotguns loaded with buckshot in case any Indians came around, and they told me they would be back whenever they could." She sighed.

"They were gone nearly three weeks, but when they returned they were driving our cattle with them. All but two yearling calves that they said the mining men had butchered for camp meat. Neither one of them ever spoke about what they had done to get those cattle back here, and I never asked. I did notice that they hadn't as much ammunition with them when they returned. But then that might have been because they had to hunt for their meat along the way. I never asked and they never said." She sighed again. "Those were hard times back then, Harrison. A man had to do for himself. Stewart and your daddy did for us. The fact that we are still here proves that they did well."

"Yes, ma'am." Stories about the past did not enthuse Harrison, and his own father had been no better than Stewart or any of the others of this country. His mother had taught him that long ago.

"After you do the chores here, Harrison, I think you should ride out and check on the stock close to home," his aunt went on. "I believe that is what Stewart would want you to do."

"Yes, ma'am," he said politely if without pleasure. The stock. Always the damned stock. Cows and bulls and steers and horses. They always came first. Ahead of books, ahead of music, ahead of the joys and the pleasures of life, the damned livestock always took precedence. "I'll go right away."

In his annoyance he left the table uncleared for his aunt to take care of and went to his room to change from shoes to boots and spurs, then to the corral to tend the damned stock there and claim a horse for the day's damned work. This time he took along a pair of saddlebags, though. Not all of the day had to be lost.

He rod his horse south at a walk, across the rolling

grass that eventually reached the stark, austere beauty—
even Harrison was touched by it, more because of his
sensitivity to beauty than from any appreciation of the
land itself—of the Flint Hills region.

The Flint Hills were still beyond the horizon, though,
and the country Harrison crossed was merely more of
the same. Short grass and baked earth. Few trees and
little water. Just grass and sky and cattle with an occasional hawk to break the monotony. In this Harrison
could find no beauty.

He rode steadily, feeling the sun on his cheek and
smelling dust and oiled leather and the sharp, warm tang
of horse sweat. He drowsed from time to time in the
deep-seated saddle that his father had ridden on the long
trails out of Texas so long before.

The cattle Harrison passed grazed in widely scattered,
self-appointed herds, a dozen here, half a hundred grouped
together a mile farther on. At least here there was little
mud for the stupid bovines to mire themselves in, which
was one of the reasons Harrison had chosen to ride in
this direction.

He paid scant attention to the cattle as he rode. The
animals he saw seemed undisturbed.

He rode south for several hours before he saw the low
bluff he had been watching for, then altered his direction
slightly to head directly toward it.

At the base of the bluff there was a cattail-ringed
pond that held water much of the year. There was no
shade but at least there was a nest of rocks where a
man could curl up in relative comfort and watch the
comings and goings of the birds and small animals and,
once in a while, the pronghorn antelope that ranged the
grasslands.

Harrison hobbled his horse and took his saddlebags
from behind the cantle. He stripped his bridle from the
animal and looped it over the saddle horn before turning
the horse loose to graze or drink or otherwise content
itself until it was wanted again. Harrison carried the
saddlebags into the low crown of rocks, stretched out
with a slab of stone for a backrest and pulled a clothbound

volume of essays from the left-hand saddlebag pocket. He was as close to contentment as he expected to come for the time being.

He must have dozed because the sun was well past the zenith when he opened his eyes with a start and wondered what sound had caught his attention. He laid a pasteboard marker into the book that was open on his lap and looked around.

There were three men mounted on short, heavily muscled horses beside the seep. One of the horses was drinking and the other two were standing in the water at its edge. Nearby, also standing in the water, were half a dozen massively built red bulls. Obviously the men were driving the bulls somewhere.

In spite of the heat of the sun Harrison felt himself go cold.

The cattle thieves? He could not be sure. He was too far away to clearly see the men's faces, much less read the brands on the flanks of the bulls.

He had the impression that he had seen the men before although he did not believe he knew them.

Neither the riders nor their horses seemed to have noticed that they were being watched. The third horse finished drinking and raised its head, muzzle dripping strings of slobber and water that caught the sunlight. One of the riders said something and the other two laughed. The sound of their laughter reached Harrison clearly although he did not hear what had been said. For some reason the sound made him shrink lower against the rocks where he lay. He did not want them to see him there.

If they were the robbers . . .

Was that the right term for it, he asked himself. No. It was robbery when the criminal faced his victim. It was theft, in this case rustling, when done outside the view of the victim. The distinction ran inanely through his mind over and over again.

If they saw him . . . If they knew he was spying on them . . .

Was he doing that? spying on them? Dammit, he was *not*, he told himself indignantly. He was perfectly innocent of any such intention. He had been here *reading*, not spying. He could prove that to them. He could show them the book. Point to the very essay. He touched the spine of the book and ran his fingers across the cloth of the binding as if the book were a talisman and a proof.

But felons would not care about that, would they? They would not, he was sure.

The fact of discovery, the fact of his being there—they might be capable of any barbaric action to protect themselves.

Harrison's breath was coming in short, rapid gasps and he opened his mouth to keep the sound of his breathing from whistling through his nose. He was sure if he kept his mouth closed the men—he was convinced by now that they were the cattle thieves—would hear him and would come for him.

Chill sweat formed on his forehead and in his armpits. The feel of its trickle was maddeningly uncomfortable, but he could not risk the movement to wipe it away. Motion was what drew attention. He had heard time and again how a hunter could lie in plain sight on the bare prairie and remain undetected so long as he remained motionless. The Indians had used that trick to waylay countless settlers in the years past. He had heard that time and time again. He did not dare move or the men were sure to discover him.

The rock slabs that had been so comfortable a few minutes earlier now felt hard and uncompromising. The stone bit into his back and his rump. It was painful. He tensed against the discomfort and could feel a cramp forming in his right thigh, but he did not dare to move to ease the cramp.

The cramp clutched at his thigh like a powerful hand, and he felt sweat form on his upper lip and roll nastily down his cheeks. Harrison gritted his teeth to guard against any outcry. His bowels felt loose and he began to be desperately afraid that he might foul himself.

Below him the men remained unaware that they were watched. One of them hooked a knee around his saddle horn, as Jesse Howard had done when they met the week past, and toyed with the rowel of his spur. Another pulled a pipe from his pocket and took his time about shaving tobacco into the bowl from a plug, tamping and lighting it. They seemed in no hurry. Harrison wished fervently that they would go away.

The cramp subsided but the pain in his lower back was extreme where the rock was cutting into him. He lay there, forcing himself to breathe shallowly, guarding against the slightest motion.

Finally—it must have been twenty minutes and seemed ten times that long—the riders took up their reins and settled themselves in their saddles, in that casual, unconscious posture of the longtime horseman.

They spoke among themselves and again their laughter reached Harrison's ears.

One of them rode deeper into the pond to move the bulls away from it while the other two, so casually that it seemed by accident rather than design, drifted into position to guide the bulls north and west.

The bulls walked slowly away in the desired direction, the horsemen seeming to follow rather than control them. Whoever the men were they knew what they were doing. The bulls would reach their destination with no loss of either weight or energy.

They moved away slowly, and Harrison bit his lip to keep himself from jumping to his feet and screaming for them to hurry. So long as they remained in sight he remained in danger. So long as they were in view there was still the possibility that one of them might turn for a look behind and spot the innocent watcher who had been spying on them.

Harrison felt a chill race up his spine and he swallowed hard to force back a gag reaction that was crawling through his throat.

None turned, though. The three men and their slowly driven bulls—someone's driven bulls—moved steadily on across the short grass.

They passed over a slight rise and down the other side, the stocky, red bulls disappearing first and then the horses until finally all Harrison could see of the men were their shoulders and hats. And then they were gone altogether.

The tension drained out of Harrison's tight shoulders and he fell back limp against the rocks. His shirt was soaked at his armpits and down the whole of his back. He felt cold.

But he was safe. And the men were gone. His knees were weak and he staggered when he went down to the pond to get a drink. He would wait at least an hour, he decided, before he looked for his horse and began the long ride home.

CHAPTER 13

Harrison liked the way Martha's dimples showed when she smiled, as she was doing now. He liked the way the curls in her hair bounced like soft, intricately fashioned springs of spun gold whenever she moved her head. He liked very nearly everything about the girl. Not nearly, he amended, everything.

"Do you have to get back to the ranch early, Harrison?"

He shook his head.

"Then why don't you stay for dinner?" Without waiting for his answer she turned toward her father, who was behind the counter several paces away. "That would be all right wouldn't it, Daddy?"

"Mmmm," her father consented. Harrison thought he could detect a slight smile in the set of the older man's lips, but he was not sure.

"You will come, won't you?"

"I would be honored," Harrison said formally.

"We close in about an hour. I'll run back and tell Mama to expect you." The Trope family lived in a house separated from but close to the store. Martha showed her dimples again, gathered her skirts and whisked through the back door out of sight.

"Thank you for the invitation, sir," Harrison said.

Trope grinned at him. "Don't thank me, son. The idea was all hers." He shook his head fondly. "A man learns quick enough when his young reach a certain age that he isn't the master of his house that he'd always thought."

"Yes, sir," Harrison said without fully understanding.

"Meantime, Harrison, is there anything I can get for you?"

"Yes, sir, there is. I came in for a few pounds of coffee." They still had a more than sufficient supply at the Running W, particularly with Stewart and his appetite for the brew absent, but Harrison had wanted some pretext to go to town. It had been boredom, not need, that lay behind the visit. Boredom and a desire to be among others. He was still unnerved by his encounter two days before with the three men and felt a need to seek out company. He had not told anyone about seeing the men and did not intend to mention it, but he felt better about the experience now that he was surrounded by the people of Redbluff. The reason for his silence he felt but did not care to examine; he simply accepted the wisdom of the decision.

"How much?" Trope asked.

"Two pounds should do it, sir."

The storekeeper nodded and scooped the dusky beans from a huge sack into the pan of his scales. "Close enough," he announced and poured them into a sack. Nelda would roast them sometime in the next few days, when her oven was already in use, and they would be ground as needed.

"Thank you, sir."

"Anytime, Harrison." Trope turned away to mark the purchase in his account book. Like most ranch families the Wilkes settled their bill at the store once or twice a year as the cash flow dictated.

Harrison had time to kill and he did not particularly want to do it under the watchful eye of Martha's father. Not that his intentions were in any way untoward. He simply felt he would be more comfortable elsewhere. He took his sack of green coffee beans and headed outside to put them in his saddlebags before he might forget them.

"Oh."

Harrison came to an abrupt halt just inside the mercantile door, his face draining of color and a feeling running through him like an arctic gust of wind had just swept in through the open doorway.

Before him were three tall men. Three rough-looking men he had seen before.

He had seen them at the dance that Saturday night.

He might also have seen them herding a half dozen bulls off the range claimed by the Running W.

"Excuse me . . ." he stammered.

The nearest of the men smiled tolerantly and nodded. "Sure thing, fella." The man wore a drooping mustache and spoke with a slow drawl. He also carried a large revolver holstered on his belly.

Harrison's eyes were drawn to the gun. He could see that the unpolished walnut of the grips was scarred and gouged. The weapon had seen much use. It looked as large as the brass cannon used during Fourth of July celebrations in the grove beside the church. It looked larger, Harrison thought.

"You know, fella," the tall man drawled, "one of us had best kinda move aside. An' I don't see as how I could do that since I'm plumb in the middle of this doorway. Would you mind?"

He was still smiling. Thank God, Harrison thought. He was still smiling.

Quickly, nervously, Harrison stepped out of the man's way and the three of them shouldered their way into the store.

"Thankya." It came out as one word.

The men went toward the store counter, ignoring Harrison, and he took the opportunity to sidle outside. He breathed much easier once there was a wall between the three men and himself.

At least, he thought rapidly, that proved that they had not seen him lying in the nest of rock. If they had any suspicions . . .

But no, he had already known that, hadn't he? They would have come for him then and there if they had had the least hint that they were observed.

Now they were in town doing their shopping, bold and brazen as brass. Open as could be about it.

Harrison puffed out his cheeks and exhaled slowly in relief.

He put the coffee beans into his saddlebags and hurried down the street. Even if those men did not suspect him, he did not want to be in their sight a moment longer than was necessary.

CHAPTER 14

Trope gave his wife and daughter an appreciative smile as they carried the dinner plates away to exchange them for coffee and dessert. "What were you saying, Harrison? Oh yes. Those boys that were in the store this afternoon." He patted his pockets in search of his pipe and matches.

"Brothers, all three of them. Up from Texas, they say. Lots of wire going up down their way, so they've moved up here to new range. They came ahead to locate, and their stockers will be following. Took up claims near the headwaters of Three Button Creek, I understand, up north of the Howard place."

"Would you, uh, say that they were men of means, Mr. Trope?"

The older man grinned at him. "How can you tell with one of those Texians? All I know is what they've told me and that they pay cash for whatever they buy. Been in the store a couple times now, and they loaded up heavy on the supplies."

"You would say then that they intend to stay?"

"I would." Trope finished loading his pipe just in time for the ladies to return with pie and coffee. He laid the pipe and matches aside for future use. "Why?"

Harrison shrugged. "Just curious. I saw them at the dance and again in the store. It seemed odd."

"Odd enough these days, I suppose. We've all been settled in here so long now that we aren't used to new-comers moving in. But of course it's still open range. No reason why somebody couldn't start up fresh here if he wants to. That's the way everybody here got his start, and not all that many years ago either."

"Yessir."

"That will be enough man talk until later," Mrs. Trope said. To Harrison she added, "Martha made this pie herself, you know."

"No, ma'am, I did not, but I will keep it in mind."

Martha blushed and turned away toward the sideboard in a futile attempt to hide it.

After the dessert Mrs. Trope collared her husband and informed him that he would be helping wipe the dishes while the "young people" occupied the parlor. Trope left his pipe on the table and went off to do his parental duty.

"That was an excellent pie, Miss Trope."

"Thank you, Mr. Wilke, I—excuse me please, I hear someone on the porch."

Harrison could hear the footsteps too. He went into the parlor to wait politely while Martha answered the door. The parlor windows were open and he could not avoid overhearing.

"I didn't expect you," Martha's voice came. He thought there was a faint edge in the tone of it.

"I thought you might." It was a man's voice, but Harrison could not immediately place it.

"You were mistaken, sir."

"Am I causing you an inconvenience?"

"I have a guest."

There was a moment of silence. "So I see. I recognize that horse, I reckon."

"Meaning what, sir?"

Another silence. "Meaning nothing, Martha. Excuse me, Miss Trope. I . . . have no right to be forward with you. Nor any desire but for your happiness. I . . . hope you do know that."

"I do not," she said snippishly.

"As you wish." The male voice was colder now, more formal. "In that case, Miss Trope, I wish you a good evening.

Harrison heard the sound of booted footsteps on the porch boards and the hollow clomp of the man descending the stairs to the ground.

Harrison glanced quickly around. There was no one else in view and he could not restrain himself from looking out the window to see who the visitor had been. He pulled the curtains aside an inch or two and peered out, cursing under his breath when he saw.

Jesse Howard. Handsome, empty-headed, rustic Jesse Howard.

Marthia Trope could do better than that, Harrison thought defiantly. Much better.

He hurried away from the window and was seated in an overstuffed armchair when the girl joined him in the parlor. He was seated a carefully long distance from the windows that opened onto the porch. He smiled happily at her appearance in the wide doorway.

CHAPTER 15

"Sons of bitches," Stewart growled. He slammed his saddlebags down onto the table and laid his rifle across them with more care.

"Are you all right?" his wife asked.

"All right? I should hope so. No reason not to be. Never got within a half day's ride of them, near as I can tell, and that was right at the start. No trail worth following and bad guesswork to boot. Damn them." Failure of any kind weighed heavily on him, and this particular failure was anything but an exception to that rule.

"Whoever they were, well, I'm not so sure now that they went on west after all. That was the way I was figuring it." He scrubbed at his dirty, unshaven cheek. "I was wrong, dammit. I was plain wrong about them. *Let* them get away. My own damn fault."

"Sit down, old mister, I'll bring you something to eat."

"I'm not hungry," he said grumpily.

"Of course you are. Now sit."

He sat.

"Harrison," Nelda said, "fetch your uncle a glass of whiskey. He needs that as much as he needs the food."

Stewart gave her an appreciative look but put none of it into words. Instead he picked up his rifle from the table in front of him and began unloading the weapon for cleaning.

Harrison set a glass of sorrel-colored whiskey before him, and Nelda swept the squat brass and lead cartridges aside to put a plate of fresh bread and cold meat

51

on the table. Stewart grunted what might have been a thank-you.

Harrison was neither surprised nor unhappy that the cattle thieves had not been caught. Not surprised because he was sure of where they had been while his uncle was miles and days away trying to find them. Not unhappy because, in spite of the fear he felt for himself when he thought about those three brothers from Texas, he simply could not countenance the idea of physical violence. Particularly hanging.

He shuddered at the very idea of a hanging.

Once, when he was no more than eleven if that old, he had witnessed a public hanging. An accepted if not entirely within the letter of the law hanging.

It had been right there in Redbluff, and Harrison remembered all too clearly that his mother had gone somewhere that day. He had no idea where she might have been when he needed her then, but instead of being under her gentle guidance he had been playing with a group of other boys about his own age. Conrad Burton had been one of them. There had been several others who Harrison could not remember now.

Formal law had been even less well established then than it was now, and the hanging was to take place on the authority of the village justice of the peace, an ancient man with a white beard and mustache and a nearly bald head. Harrison could remember exactly what the old geezer had looked like but could no longer recall his name.

The boys, the entire town, had known about the hanging. It was to be one of the major social events of the year, and spectators had driven in from great distances to picnic in the grove—there had been no church there at that time—and watch a scarecrow figure known as Beartrap hang by the neck until dead, for the crime of murder. It had been his own woman, presumably his wife, that he had chopped up one winter in the isolation of their soddy.

Harrison could remember wondering at the time about the condemned man's name. There were no bears within half a week's ride of Redbluff and never had been in the memory of anyone living.

But he had no desire at all to actually see Beartrap hang for his crime.

Conrad and the other boys had insisted. When the time came for Beartrap to be produced from the root cellar that was doubling as the town jail, Harrison ignored their taunts and ran for home.

They called him names, he remembered, but that was not particularly unusual. That was also before he became friendly with Conrad Burton. Odd that he would have forgotten that, but he had.

He ran and behind his back they ran along after him, calling him *mama's boy* and *tweedledee*, which for some reason was supposed to be viciously derogatory at the time, and certain terms appropriate to the feminine gender. He ignored them and ran.

They caught him, though, Conrad and another boy. Willie, it had been. Willie Cutchell. He remembered now. Willie Cutchell, who died when he was fifteen or so, kicked in the head by a mule while he was trying to play a prank on the wagon's owner. But Willie had been very much alive the day the man called Beartrap died, and it was Willie and Conrad who grabbed the screaming, kicking and very soon bawling Harrison by the arms and dragged him out to where the crowd was assembled for the hanging.

All the townspeople had been there except for Harrison's gentle mother and very, very few others. The gathering was as large as for the Fourth of July, and two politicians from Trentsville drove over to deliver stirring addresses condemning sin and supporting righteousness. Harrison should have been fascinated. Instead he felt sick to his stomach.

When the speechmaking was done and a circuit preacher—that was before Bernard Cale came to Redbluff—delivered a benediction, the ancient justice of the peace was helped onto the gallows platform to read in a loud, clear voice his verdict and sentence. Half a dozen men of the community, unashamed and their faces uncovered, marched Beartrap up the thirteen steps to the platform.

They had had to carry him most of the way, lifting him under his arms as his knees were buckled and wobbly.

He was a stringy, lean man dressed in clothing little better than rags, and the impression he gave being taken up those steps was more than ever that of a scarecrow. He was pale, his mouth hanging open and a thin stream of drool running down his jaw, and he might well have died of fright if they had not been quick about the hanging.

Someone, Harrison thought it might have been Luther MacRae, who later became the constable, put the noose over Beartrap's head while two other men held him upright.

The trap door was sprung before anyone thought to tell the men supporting Beartrap to release him, and they found themselves holding him aloft over an empty hole in the platform. Harrison clearly remembered the look of astonishment the two men passed. Then, ludicrously, they jostled the poor, terrified fellow up and down as if they were playing with a tot, counting aloud "one-two-three." On the count of three they released their hold under Beartrap's arms and let him fall.

Harrison winced at the memory.

No one in Redbluff really knew how to conduct a hanging—it was hardly something they would have experience with—and the length of the drop was too short for the scrawny criminal's weight, nor had the bulky hangman's knot been placed under his ear so that the snap and the bulk would pop his neck and let him die cleanly and quickly.

Worse, no one had thought to provide a hood so that the crowd would not have to witness the effects of the hanging in the dying man's expressions.

He jolted to a stop at the end of the rope but he was not yet dead and he kicked his legs like a headless chicken, and the combination of pulling noose and dying contortions drew his face into a hideous mask that quickly colored red and soon purple. His eyes bulged and his tongue protruded from his mouth, and within seconds there was a dark, wet stain down the front of his ragtag trousers and another stain in the back as he voided himself.

Harrison never did know when the poor man actually died. Before that happened Harrison was down on his knees in the dirt, vomiting in choked spasms between sobs.

The other boys, who had insisted that Harrison watch, looked to be acutely uncomfortable too except for Willie Cutchell, who had been laughing at the way Beartrap's legs jerked.

The experience had stayed with Harrison through the years, was still with him, and it was one he hoped never to see repeated. Or to know of.

If that meant that his uncle had to lose a few head of cattle without the satisfaction of revenge then so be it.

Harrison was not at all displeased that his uncle had come back angry and unsatisfied.

He shook his head when his aunt offered him a snack while Stewart ate. He had no appetite. The memory of that long-ago hanging was much too strong.

Harrison shuddered and left the table for the privacy of his room.

CHAPTER 16

Stewart and Harrison reached Redbluff far quicker than Harrison normally did at his slow, cautious gait yet almost as rapidly as the hands were able to do at their normal, breakneck pace. The horses were sweated but not lathered and again it amazed Harrison that the aging rancher could get so much out of an animal without seeming to take much out of it. Stewart brought them to a halt in front of the better of the town's two saloons and motioned for Harrison to get down.

"Should I—?"

"No, doddammit, you stick with me this time. You can get your mail later. I swear, boy, if I let you get your hands on one of them eastern papers now you wouldn't have your nose outta it 'til you run out of lamp oil." Stewart had remained angry every moment since he got back. Even touchier than usual, Harrison thought, which was considerable to begin with.

He stepped down from the horse and aped his uncle in tying the reins of his horse—a rather too spirited selection this time but necessary if he expected to keep up with Stewart on the road—to the rail secured along the wooden sidewalk.

Harrison trailed his uncle through the open, bead-hung doorway into the dim and relatively cool interior of the saloon.

Odors, most of them offensive, surrounded him as soon as they were inside. There was the sharp but not objectionable scent of fresh beer. Beyond that, though, were the stink of sweat and vomit and stale tobacco and long-unwashed spittoons. Harrison wrinkled his nose but refrained from making any comment.

It was early afternoon and the place was busy if not actually crowded. Half a dozen men leaned over glass mugs at the bar and perhaps a quarter of the tables were filled. There were no card games in progress at such an early hour but most of the customers had plates or papers at their elbows, piled with offerings from the free lunch that was spread at the far end of the bar.

Stewart Wilke nodded his way through the place to the free lunch, took a plate for himself and handed one to Harrison. He began loading the small plate with mounds of ham and pickled sausages and pickled pigeon eggs and heavily salted crackers. Harrison was more selective, not caring much for the salt-cured ham and sour sausages. He selected a few crackers and one egg and waited for his uncle to finish.

"This way," Stewart ordered when his plate would hold no more. He elbowed through the men, Harrison following meekly behind, to a table in the front corner where the same group of men spent several hours each and every afternoon of the workweek.

"Boys," Stewart greeted them.

The men who returned that juvenile greeting were each at least as old as Stewart and most of them showed more gray in their hair than dark. All but one were wearing suits for their workaday clothing.

There were three. The oldest and most elegantly dressed was W. Charles Holton, president and owner of the Redbluff Bank of Commerce. At his left, also well dressed, was Tom Yates, part-time lawyer and part-time real estate developer, full-time landlord over much of the town's property. The third man, wearing a vest and sleeve garters but no coat, was Jason Taylor, freighter and merchant and chairman of the local Republican. committee.

Among them the three controlled the incorporated limits of Redbluff, while Stewart Wilke, Vance Howard and a very few others were the he-coons of its environs.

Stewart took a seat at their table without needing to wait for an invitation. He motioned for Harrison to sit in a chair at the adjacent vacant table. The secondary position, as if he were no more than a hired hand, rankled. For another rancher, even Vance Howard, who Stewart detested, room would have been made at the table.

Michael McMichael brought a pair of clean mugs and a fresh pitcher of beer from behind the bar even though it was too early in the day for table service. Harrison accepted his and drank from it, wanting to refuse it and ask instead for a lemonade or soft drink, knowing that he would not, hating the fact that he continued to try to act the way his uncle thought he should and not as he really wanted. He took another swallow of the sour stuff and kept his face impassive.

"It isn't usual to see you in here this time of day," one of the men was saying.

Stewart grunted.

"We heard you were off looking for some rustlers," Holton said.

"Didn't find 'em," Stewart grumped. "Smart sons of bitches."

"They must have been."

Wilke grunted again. "I don't s'pose our respectable sheriff's been heard from." His tone of voice made it more complaint than question.

"Of course he has been," Taylor said soothingly. The party chairman reached to refill Stewart's mug. "He asked for full particulars about the matter. Not just your loss, Stew, but Vance Howard's too. The sheriff is deeply concerned."

"I'll bet," Wilke said. His voice was heavily laced with sarcasm. He wrapped a meaty hand around his mug, ignoring the handle, and took a long pull at it that nearly drained it. "Well, I didn't expect anything better, an' that's a fact. Deep concern, boys, but no action. Still, a man has to try."

"Don't worry about it, Stewart," Holton said. "More than likely it was just a bunch of cowboys passing through and picking up some extra money. Lord knows, you can afford the loss."

Wilke grunted.

Any of the men at the table had a good idea of how many beeves Stewart Wilke's Running W had, but the banker knew the figure precisely. As precisely as any man could count when cattle are run on open range, anyway. A breakdown of Running W cows, steers, yearling heifers and breeder bulls would be on Holton's books. Only the calf crop would be missing, and those could be closely estimated.

"It isn't the money," Stewart said.

"We know that," Yates told him.

"What I'm wondering, with Howard and me both missing stock, is if we got ourselves a problem here."

"I wouldn't think so," Yates said. He sounded unconcerned.

"Course you wouldn't, Tom. No son of a bitch can up and walk off with your assets like they can mine. Maybe you don't remember how things used to be around here, but I do. Don't want it to go back to that neither."

"None of us wants that," Taylor said.

Harrison had no idea what they were talking about. Whatever it was it must have happened before his time.

"You haven't heard of any more losses then, boys?" Stewart asked.

The three men looked at each other. They shook their heads. "I tell you, Stewart, it was probably just some loose-footed boys passing through with big thirsts and long ropes. Don't worry about it."

Stewart looked unconvinced, but he nodded his head. "Just thought I'd ask." He finished his beer. "An', Tom. You send a note over to the sheriff. If this turns out to be more than what Charlie thinks, well, we'll be handling it the way it has to be. With him or without, it's got to be done. Make sure he knows that, Tom."

"I will, Stew. I'll write to him this afternoon if you want."

"That's exactly what I'd want." He stood and without turning to look at Harrison said, "C'mon, boy."

Harrison hurried after his long-striding uncle. With any luck he would have a few minutes to visit with Martha when he went to pick up their mail.

CHAPTER 17

Tim, the older of their two full-time hands and Harrison's favorite, if he could be said to prefer one of the cowboys over the other, met them at the corral gate when they loped in at Stewart's easy, ground-eating pace. The man looked worried. And it was unusual for either of the hands to meet Wilke at the gate. Boss and ranch owner or not, it would have occurred to none of them that Stewart should not do his own unsaddling.

"Evenin', Stew," Tim drawled.

Harrison never had accepted the hired hands' familiarity with their betters. The only reason he preferred Tim over the second hand, Albert, was that at least Tim could read. Albert apparently could not; certainly he did not.

"You look awful down in the mouth." Stewart stepped down from his horse and pulled the saddle, dumping it into the dust and dried manure of the corral. He took an ancient and almost bristleless brush from the top of a fence post and began to rub his horse down. Over his shoulder, without having to look in Harrison's direction, he growled, "Don't you be running off without cleaning that animal's back, you hear?"

"Yessir." Harrison reluctantly did as he was told. That was a standing rule at the Running W, if one he commonly ignored when he was alone.

"Now what was it you were wanting, Tim?"

"More trouble, Stew."

Wilke stopped what he was doing and leaned across the back of his horse, waiting for the cowboy to continue.

"I rode down the south end of the graze today, Stew."

Wilke nodded.

"You know that bunch of twos we got down there."

Again Stewart nodded. Twos were two-year-old steers that would be ready for marketing as beef on the hoof in the fall. That, as with so much else in the business, had changed in recent years. Once a steer was not deemed fit for slaughter until it was at least five years old and preferably seven. Now the beeves were sold as three-year-olds or "long twos" approaching that age.

"There's some of 'em missing."

Wilke did not ask if Tim was sure. The man would not have said it if he were not certain. "How many?"

Tim shrugged. "I ain't positive. Some could of dropped out of the bunch while we was gone. But there's twenny-eight head less than the last time I seen them."

"I don't suppose they could all have drifted out," Stewart mused aloud.

"I checked for a good ways around," Tim said. "That brindle that dewlapped himself by accident that time an' the snotty little red with the crooked right horn, they're both out of the country for sure. Couldn't miss either of them two from any distance."

Stewart accepted the statement as a form of proof. And Harrison had to agree. He would never, he was sure, understand how a person was expected to differentiate one bovine animal from another when there were hundreds of the things carrying the Running W brand, but the fact was that Stewart and either of the hands could describe one individual cow and both other men would know exactly which one they were talking about.

"Twenty-eight, huh?"

" 'Bout that."

"Tracks?"

Tim shook his head. "Not that I seen, but then I didn't hang around an' look all that hard. Soon as I figured what was what I fogged it back here to tell you when you got in."

"All right then," Stewart said wearily. It was a rare sign of weakness for him. He took his broad-brimmed hat off and resettled it while for a brief moment he stared blankly down toward the ground. When he looked up again his shoulders were straighter and his voice once again crisp and decisive.

"Boy, go tell your aunt we're riding out again for a spell. Bring along a sack of groceries and your bedroll. A gun too, I think."

"I don't wa—"

"When I wanta know what you *want*, boy, I'll ask," Stewart snapped. "You bring that shotgun that stands by my desk. And mind you don't shoot yourself with it. It's loaded. Tim, you go tell Albert what we're up to. He can stay here an' keep an eye on the north end o' the place a bit."

Tim nodded and was heading for the bunkhouse soddy before Harrison could swallow back the anger that was churning inside him.

His uncle had no right to speak to him like that in front of the help, he raged in silence. No right at all.

There was nothing for him to do, though, but to comply. He turned the horse he had been riding loose to mingle with the others in the corral, lifted his saddle onto a rail and went off at a deliberately casual speed to perform the errand.

CHAPTER 18

Harrison was miserable. Sleeping on the ground was bad enough, but Stewart had made them ride for hours through the darkness until they reached the area where the steers apparently had been taken.

"Apparent" was the key word there, Harrison reminded himself. Just because Tim had not been able to locate a particular steer or two was no reason to assume that they had been stolen as far as he was concerned. Certainly it was not worth this kind of misery.

A very few hours of sleep on a very hard area of stony soil and now Stewart was breaking camp in the dim, gray predawn without so much as a fire and a pot of coffee to drive the chill out of aching muscles. It was both unfair and unnecessary, Harrison felt. Tim said himself that he found no tracks for them to follow. And if any cattle had been stolen—*if* any were—there was no way to know how long ago it might have been.

So why the big hurry? Harrison pulled his boots back on over clammy, sweat-damp socks that he had been wearing for more than a day and night now and groaned his way onto his feet.

"Roll your bed now, boy, and doddammit don't leave your shotgun laying there like that." Stewart stomped over to Harrison's bed and picked up the double-barreled shotgun that Harrison had tossed onto the ground beside him when he went to sleep a few hours earlier.

The older man upended the barrels and shook the gun as if he expected a peck of pebbles to come tumbling out. Harrison would not have cared if the thing had been full of dirt and stones; he had no intention of using it in any event.

"Hurry up, dammit."

"Yessir." Both Tim and Stewart, he saw, already had their beds rolled and tied, and Tim had already limped off—Harrison was slightly mollified to see that the cowboy too seemed to be stiff this morning—to find the horses and bring them up to the makeshift camp.

Both of the others were saddled and bridled by the time Harrison had his gear together and his eyes more or less open. He saddled hastily, not liking the way his horse rolled its eyes and pinned its ears back in the first rose-colored light of the early morning.

"Are you coming with us?" Stewart demanded.

"Yessir." Harrison pulled his cinches tight and lifted his foot to the stirrup. The horse rolled its eyes again and sidestepped neatly away from him. "I'm coming," Harrison said quickly before his uncle could object.

The other two were already mounted, and Stewart gave Harrison a coldly impatient glare.

Harrison tried for the stirrup again and again the hammerheaded horse stepped away from him.

"Cheek him, dammit."

"I'm trying," Harrison said. He had not been, and they all knew it.

He pulled the near rein to draw the horse's head around toward the stirrup, but once again the animal sidestepped away from Harrison's raised foot.

Either of the men could have reined close enough to hold the edgy horse's head until Harrison could get into the saddle, but neither man did so. They sat watching him, Tim's face impassive and Stewart's openly contemptuous.

Harrison tried to mount yet again. This time when the horse sidled away his exasperation reached a boiling point and he lashed out into the animal's belly with the sharply pointed toe of his riding boot. The horse walled its eyes and threw its head. But the next time Harrison tried to mount it stood still for him.

"That's more like it," Stewart said with a grunt. " 'Bout time you learned."

Still angry, Harrison booted the horse hard in the ribs

to get him moving although a shift of weight and a tightening of his knees would have been enough.

The horse was apparently as angry as its rider. Its ears flew back tight against its skull, and it bogged its head. Harrison had time enough to see the quick grin reach his uncle's face when he saw what was coming.

Harrison grabbed instinctively for the saddle horn—the hell with the fancy niceties of riding—and felt the saddle begin to seesaw as the horse bucked and reared. Harrison clamped down on its barrel with his legs and concentrated on staying upright. With his rein hand he yanked savagely at the bit, trying to bring the animal under control and keep its head up so it could not pitch.

The horse threw its head up just as Harrison was flung forward by a slam of its forelegs into the ground. The horse's poll smashed Harrison in the face. His mouth and nose felt numb.

He was aware that off to the side Tim was shouting encouragement, although to him or to the horse he was not sure. He released his hold on the horn long enough to hit the animal over the skull with a clubbed fist, then grabbed for his handhold again. He heard Tim give out a high-pitched yip.

The horse brought all four hooves back down to the ground and tried to bolt. Harrison snatched back on the reins with all his strength, not really caring if he tore the horse's mouth or not. The animal's head flew up again, and Harrison felt himself rising into the air to an unnatural height.

"Get off his mouth, doddammit," Stewart shouted, but it was already too late.

The horse was rearing, coming up on its hind legs with its forefeet pawing the air.

Alone it would have been fine, but with the weight of saddle and rider on its back the horse overbalanced. It pawed the air and duck-walked backward, trying to regain the lost balance, but it was too late for that.

"Quit 'im!" Stewart yelled.

Harrison heard but the meaning was not immediately clear to him. Quit what? he wanted to ask. He turned his head to look toward Stewart and he felt the horse begin its tumble backward.

He threw himself to the side, knowing that his boots were still socketed deep into the stirrups, knowing that he had no chance at all to jump free before the horse fell over backward with half a ton of crushing force striking the hard ground.

Harrison's shoulders hit the ground first and then the back of his head. He felt a brief flash of sharp pain and then nothing at all.

CHAPTER 19

"You were lucky." It was the consensus among those who came to visit him. It was also the truth.

Harrison, though, did not feel particularly lucky. His head still ached fearsomely, both from the blow he had taken there and from the more recent and much better remembered agony of the split in his scalp being sewed together by Joe Crane, who was Redbluff's barber, physician and veterinarian.

His gut hurt from where the damned horse had rolled on him. It hurt even though people kept reminding him how very fortunate he was that the saddle horn had not caught him and crushed his chest or punctured his insides. That could happen all too easily and did happen all too often.

He hurt from head to toe and was told—his neck was much too stiff and sore for him to raise his head and see for himself—that he was bruised black and purple over most of his body.

Still, they kept telling him how lucky he was that there seemed to be no serious damage and that nothing was broken.

Harrison did not feel lucky in the slightest.

The trip into town had been one long, agonized blur of motion and pain, carried on the back of the same damned horse that had almost killed him, Tim leading the animal and Harrison clinging to its back with his face a contorted mask and whimpering groans being forced through his clenched teeth with every footfall the horse made. He could not remember all of the trip and did not want to. Stewart was still out there somewhere looking for his lost steers.

Damn *him*, Harrison thought. He didn't even know if Harrison was alive or dead. Harrison's guts could have been punctured and he could have been dying for all Stewart knew, but that had made no difference to him. He had sent Harrison back with a hired hand and went on by himself to tend to the more important business of a few dollars' worth of missing livestock.

Harrison detested him. At the moment Harrison detested very nearly everything and everyone in and around Redbluff.

A wave of pain washed over him, and he arched his back against it. The stiffening of his muscles was even more painful and he cried out, not caring if anyone heard or not. Stoic acceptance of acute pain was all right for those too ignorant to feel pain; it was not for him.

"Mighty lucky," Conrad Burton repeated. Harrison did not try to correct him.

"Tim said he'd borrow a wagon to carry you back to the house."

"No."

"What?"

"I said—" Harrison stopped for a moment and winced. "I said no. I don't want to be bounced around in a damn wagon. Not for a while yet."

"Tim's already gone to borrow the wagon."

"He can just unborrow it then. I'm not going anywhere for a while."

Con shrugged.

"Do me a favor, would you?"

"Of course."

"Ask Bernard Cale if I could sleep over at his place for a few days. Until I'm feeling up to traveling. Would you do that?"

"Of course, but what about your uncle?"

"I don't *care* about my damned uncle, Con. And that is the truth. I just want to lie down and sleep for about a week. I never wanted to go out with him anyway. Crazy old man." Harrison closed his eyes and tried to will himself to not stiffen against the pain that was sweeping through him. That only made it worse.

"Whatever you say, Harrison." Burton left the barber

shop, where Harrison was laid out on a folding cot, and Harrison watched him go, envying the cleanliness and relative civility, even here in Redbluff, that Conrad was exposed to day in and day out. He never had to put up with hidebound old men who had outlived their time or with half-broken horses and heat and rain and sweat and misery, Harrison thought.

There was the sound of a wagon rolling to a halt beyond the barber shop doorway, and a moment later Tim came inside.

"Joe says I can take you home now." No greeting, no sympathy, just that.

"I'm not going."

"What?"

"I said I'm not going." Harrison swallowed and had an idea. "Uncle Stewart might need you out there, Tim. I'll be all right here. I can stay with Bernard Cale. Or anybody if he can't take me in. You get straight on back to where you left my uncle. You don't know, Tim. He might be in trouble by himself if he finds those thieves. Don't worry about me, now. Just get on back to him, you hear?"

"Damned if I expected you to be that way about it, Harrison." The hired hand grinned at him. "Hell, I thought you'd be mousin' around cryin' and carryin' on and here you're worried 'bout Stew. That's all right, boy." The cowboy clapped him familiarly on the shoulder, sending a fresh gout of pain through Harrison's frame and bringing a wave of anger with it, but he controlled himself and forced himself to grin back at the ignoramus.

"That's the way I feel about it, Tim."

"I'll tell him you said so."

"You do that."

Tim touched his hat brim in a salute of sorts and hurried back outside. The gesture surprised Harrison and touched him. None of the hired men, full-time or transients, had ever been pleasant to him before. Certainly none had ever shown him any form of respect. If that was what Tim's gesture had been. He wondered. And decided it probably was not.

Not that he cared. All Harrison Wilke wanted from Redbluff and its citizens was *from*. As in "away from."

He lay very still on Joe Crane's cot and tried not to provoke any more pain in his bruised and battered body.

CHAPTER 20

"You have a mighty attentive nurse," Bernard Cale said with a smile as he hunched over the board between them. "Not that I'm complaining, mind you. As long as she brings enough for both of us, the young lady is more than welcome." Almost absently the preacher used a forefinger to nudge his rook ahead two squares. The move gave protection to one of his own bishops and placed Harrison's queen in jeopardy within another two moves.

"You're trying to distract me," Harrison said accusingly.

"I am *not*." Cale rolled his eyes and mimed a look of great piety and innocence.

Harrison withdrew a developing attack and pulled his bishop back in defense of his queen.

Martha Trope had come by the Cale house at least twice daily since Harrison had been brought into town, at least once in the forenoon with a cold dinner for the two of them and again in the evening with pie or fudge or some such delicacy. Usually she stayed to talk while the preacher discreetly found urgent chores to occupy him elsewhere in the small house. This evening the offering had been brownies. There were little more than crumbs left on the plate beside the chessboard.

"You seem to be moving comfortably again, Harrison."

"I'm getting better," he agreed.

"I'm glad to hear that." Cale continued to study the board.

"There is still a great deal of pain," Harrison said. He advanced a knight, withdrew his hand and only then realized that he had made an error. He reached for the small wooden figure and picked it up. "Would you mind?"

"Go ahead."

Harrison replaced the knight where it had been and moved a pawn instead. Technically speaking he should not have done that. Once his hand was removed from the piece he was committed to the move. But Bernard Cale did not seem to mind a loose interpretation of the rules.

"They are saying in town that your aunt needs help out at the ranch," Cale said, still looking at the board rather than at his opponent.

"Really?"

"I understand she is worried about Stewart. It has been, what, almost three weeks now?"

"Two and a half," Harrison corrected.

"Stewart hasn't gotten back, in any event. She sent both riders out to look for him. They haven't come back either. So she is alone out there now."

"Where did you hear that?"

"George Hudson. He stopped there yesterday to reset a loose shoe and stayed for coffee. He says she sounded worried and looked very tired."

"I'm sure she is all right."

Harrison had been concentrating on the expected bishop-rook attack and had forgotten about Cale's other bishop. Now the preacher slid that piece through the square just vacated by Harrison's white pawn and captured his queen. Harrison bit back an exclamation of disgust and tipped his king over, conceding the game.

"Are you sure? You still have a game if you buckle down to it."

"I'm sure."

"All right." Cale began to remove the pieces from the board, laying them into a small chest with velvet padded slots for each tiny figure. "If you want to go back home," he said while he worked, "I could get someone to drive you out tomorrow."

"I'm still pretty sore," Harrison said.

"I know." He paused. "I just thought you might want to know that people are beginning to talk."

"They can't feel what I feel. I'm still in pain, Bernard. I've told you that before."

"You needn't explain anything to me, friend Harrison."

Harrison made a sour face. "Probably any one of them would have been back in the saddle the next morning. Is that what they are saying?"

"Of course not. They are concerned about your aunt. That's all."

"They don't understand," Harrison said bitterly. "Sometimes I wonder if any of them have any feelings. They all act so tough and seem to think it a crime if other people are sensitive to pain. Sometimes, Bernard, I think they have no more feelings than a brute animal."

"Everyone feels pain, Harrison," Cale said gently. "No one has a monopoly on that."

"I wonder." He sighed. "They don't act like it, you know. None of them. They have no more sensitivity than a cow does. Less. They are considerate of cows. It is only people that they care nothing about."

"You don't believe that any more than I do, Harrison," Cale said in a soft voice. "They are trying to be considerate of your aunt. Truly."

"Dammit, Bernard . . ." Harrison gave his friend a look of helpless frustration. "I'm sorry. It just seems, sometimes, that no matter what I go through, no one here will ever understand it or care. None of them."

"None?" Cale smiled.

"Well. There might be an exception." Harrison gave him a weak smile in return.

"Even two?" Cale lightly fingered the plate with its litter of chocolate crumbs.

Harrison shrugged. "Perhaps two then."

"Three?"

"I couldn't think of a third."

"I can." Cale's voice was very gentle.

"Name him."

"Her," he corrected. "Nelda Wilke. She cares enough to take on quite a burden in your absence."

"You are telling me that you think I should go back out to that miserable place in spite of the pain, is that it?"

Cale shook his head. "It is not my place to tell you anything, Harrison. You are welcome to stay here as long as you need. I am only providing food for thought. Not suggestions; certainly not demands. You can come or go as you please."

Harrison sighed. "All right, Bernard. Tomorrow. Find me a buggy and driver if you please. I'll do what is expected of me."

"I would rather you do what you expect of yourself, Harrison."

"If I did that, Bernard . . ." Harrison spread his hands. He shook his head and said, "I just don't know what that might be. I really do not."

Cale closed the small chest and latched it shut. He stood and laid a hand on Harrison's shoulder. "Follow your heart, Harrison. Make sure you are at peace with the Lord and then follow your heart. That is all any of us can do when you come right down to it." He brightened. "Now if you can hobble your way over to that sofa, I'll go make us a pot of tea before we turn in for the night." He turned and left the room.

CHAPTER 21

The cowboy took his hat off before he stepped through the door into the kitchen. He bobbed his head nervously toward Nelda and cleared his throat several times.

Harrison looked at the man—little more than a boy, really, but considered a man because he was hired to do a man's job—with barely concealed distaste. Albert could neither read nor write, and apparently he had no desire to learn. Yet on horseback, in motion, he had a natural, fluid grace and economy of movement that made him seem a part of the nearly wild animals he preferred for his mounts. His life seemed to consist of hard, dawn-to-dusk work interspersed with occasional bouts of drunkenness and debauchery. Harrison considered Albert to be typical—and an indictment—of the type of uneducated, unambitious male this country produced. Harrison turned his head away and gave his attention to the breakfast dishes he was wiping dry.

"Par'n me, ma'am, but Tim ast me to come in."

"Is everything all right, Albert? Is Stewart all right?" She sounded deeply worried but she was already in motion, preparing a meal for the dust-covered and obviously weary hand.

"Yes'm. That is, we don't know for sure but we don't know otherwise neither."

"I don't understand." Nelda put a plate and steaming cup of coffee on the table and began pulling more plates of leftovers from the food safe.

"No'm." Albert rubbed the back of his neck and looked uncomfortable.

"Is Tim with Stewart?"

"Well . . . no, ma'am, he ain't. Exactly."

"Sit down, Albert. Please."

The cowboy did as he was told, first hanging his hat on a peg near the back door where Stewart's hat usually hung, then carefully brushing his trousers before he sat in the wooden chair. The effort created a small cloud of yellow-red dust that fell unheeded to the clean-swept floor Nelda demanded in her kitchen.

"Tell me what you have been doing. Please."

"Yes, ma'am." He took a deep, quick swallow of the scalding coffee, and Harrison winced just from watching him, yet Albert seemed not to notice the heat. "That tastes awful good, ma'am. Thank you."

She nodded and waited for him to tell her in his own time and his own way.

"We ain't exactly found your husband yet, ma'am." He glanced up with what must have been intended to be a reassuring look while he broke a biscuit open and slathered it thick with butter from the crockery tub before him. "But we can't be real awful far behind him neither."

Nelda nodded. She took a chair at the table and sat with her hands folded in her lap. Only a slow wringing of her fingers within the concealing cloth of her apron displayed her nervousness.

"We started out lookin' where Tim last seen him, you see, an' went west an' then north from there. Figured he'd leave us some sign iffn he'd went that way, but we never found none. That took more'n a few days right there." Albert pushed the biscuit into his mouth and gulped it hurriedly out of the way. He began to butter another.

"Then we rode up north, ma'am, thinkin' whoever took them cows might of crossed the Howard place. Found a campsite up that way that was sure-God Stewart's." He paused again for a mouthful of food.

Harrison snorted softly and in a skeptical tone of voice asked, "How can you be so sure it was Uncle Stewart's camp?"

Albert gave him an annoyed look. "Ain't you ever seen the way Stewart lays up his fahr? Lays the sticks in sorta catercornered while most either lay 'em crossways or teepee style. An' you, we can always tell yours. You just toss 'em in ever' which way.''

Harrison felt like he had been rebuked although he was not entirely sure of that. He folded his arms and leaned back against the dry sink, peering at Albert down the length of his nose.

"Anyway, ma'am, there wasn't no messages left or nothing like that, though he must of known we'd be coming along behind. But that told us we was going the right direction finally, so we went on up that way. Crossed Willow Run just above the bogs an' seen a blaze that might of been left for us to follow, so we kept on that way. Then yesterday we come up on a Runnin' W cow, one o' the missin' steers it was for sure, with a rope snagged on its horns. Stewart's rope, it was.''

Albert gave Harrison a hard look that had no hint of servility in it. " 'Fore you ask, we tooken the rope off the cow. The hondo's wrapped an' laced the way Stewart likes for them big loops o' his. Wrapped near clean around and real heavy. It's his, all right.

"Anyway, ma'am, we was still pretty far behind 'cause that rope had been drug around long enough to be stomped and wore short to a nubbin. But we're on the right track now an' if we can stay out long enough an' maybe find another mark or two, we'll catch up to him, Tim figures.'' Albert took a chunk of cold beef and wrapped a crumbling slab of day-old bread around it.

"The thing is, ma'am, we're most out of eatables, an' Tim figured it'd be better for me to come back here an' let you know what we're about than to go off an' borry some somewheres. So I'm to tell you an' get something to eat an' a packhorse an' meet Tim on east an' north from Spotted Horse Butte. With any luck he'll of caught up with Stewart by then an' we can get on with things.'' Albert leaned down close to his plate so the bread crumbs would not fall down his shirt and took a huge bite of his sandwich.

"Thank you, Albert,'' Nelda said. "It was good of you and Tim to think of me.''

Albert washed the dry beef and bread down with a draught of coffee and swallowed hard. "It was Tim that thought of it mostly, ma'am. He knowed you'd be fretting."

She managed a smile. "There have been worse times. You boys do what you have to do, and don't think about me again. You find Stewart and help him."

"We figure to, ma'am. God willin', we figure to do exactly that."

"Do you want to sleep a few hours before you leave again? You look like you rode all night long."

Albert grinned at her. "Like the man says, ma'am, I can sleep come winter. I'll jus' catch up some fresh horses an' be ready to go."

"Harrison, fetch me the panniers for the packsaddle." To Albert she added, "Your supplies will be ready when you are."

"Thank you, ma'am. An' thanks for the breakfast too." He grinned at her again. "Me an' Tim make out but you couldn't call neither of us a cook. That there was almighty good, ma'am." Abruptly he spun gracefully out of his chair and toward the doorway. Harrison hurried out behind him to bring in the panniers his aunt had asked for.

CHAPTER 22

Harrison felt a pleasant sense of anticipation, even though a man had come to a poor pass when he was pleased with the prospect of going into Redbluff. Because he was still a little sore here and there, and because he was not yet ready to relinquish Martha's sympathies, he had chosen to drive into town rather than ride.

He might have preferred a snappier rig to arrive in. The paint on the wheel spokes was flaked nearly away, the wooden poles were weathered gray and etched with surface cracks and the harness needed oiling. All were sure indications that Stewart Wilke thought little of driving rigs. And Harrison was unlikely to volunteer for the work. Still, he would have liked to have arrived in a vehicle much grander than this.

With a twinge of regret he wheeled the aging, cold-blooded buggy horse to a stop in front of the mercantile, got down and clipped the lead of the hitching weight to the horse's bit.

"Good afternoon, sir," Harrison said with a polite touch of his hat brim as he entered the store. He looked around the small space, but Leon Trope was the only person he could see.

"Hello, Harrison." Martha's father automatically pulled an accumulation of newspapers and magazines from Harrison's postal box and piled them onto the counter. He looked over Harrison's shoulder toward the rig parked outside. "Don't tell me you were expecting to go for a drive too."

"Sir?"

"You weren't expecting to take Martha for a drive, were you?"

"No, sir." Harrison's slight limp became more pronounced as he crossed the store to the counter. He picked up his mail. "I hope she is not feeling poorly."

"Not at all. I gave her the afternoon off so she could go for a drive."

"Really?" Harrison managed to keep himself from showing the scowl that threatened to twist his features in an unseemly display.

"About an hour ago," Trope said with some satisfaction. "She packed a basket and drove out with Jesse Howard for the afternoon." Harrison was sure the man had emphasized the name.

Damn him, Harrison thought. If control of the Running W ever left Stewart Wilke, by damn, there would be some changes in the ranch purchasing if Harrison had to do his buying out of Trentsville and pay the difference in the freight out of his own pocket.

"I am sure they are having a fine time," he said pleasantly. "It is a lovely day for a drive."

"So I see. If I had any sense at all I'd have made her tend the counter here while *I* went for a jaunt." Trope laughed. "But if you can't have fun when you're young, I always say, you never will get around to it."

"Yes, sir, I'm sure you are right about that." He touched his hat brim again. "Please give my highest regards to Mrs. Trope and to Martha, sir."

"I'll do that, Harrison. Count on it."

That would be the day, Harrison thought bitterly. The old fart. He was no better and no more sincere than any of the rest of them. With a smile and a nod he turned and left the store.

Now what? he asked himself. He had had the afternoon all planned in his mind, including a walk through the grove to the stream with Martha on his elbow. Civilized conversation and civilized pursuits for a change. Now the entire, wasted afternoon stretched bleakly before him with all his plans shattered. To turn around and drive back to the ranch and a lonely evening under the reading lamp was unthinkable.

There was always Bernard Cale, he thought. At least the preacher was a civil human being among these clods. He left the buggy parked where it was and set off down the street on foot, still limping.

"Harrison!"

"What?" He smiled. "Hello, Conrad."

The affable bank clerk was a few feet distant on the board sidewalk. He took Harrison by the elbow and steered him down into the dust of the street and across it toward the saloon.

"Come with me, Harrison. I have to have someone to celebrate with. And I won't take no for an answer. That's a fact."

"What are we celebrating?"

"Wealth, my friend. A good start toward it, in any event," Burton said with an infectious grin.

"I couldn't refuse to celebrate that, could I?"

Harrison allowed himself to be seated at a table across the room from the trio of town leaders, Holton and Yates and Taylor.

"I'm buying," Con insisted, "and I won't take no for an answer about that either." He went to the bar without asking what Harrison wanted and returned with a pair of whiskey-filled glasses.

"This must be an occasion," Harrison said. The usual daytime beverage was a beer or two.

"It would've been champagne if there was any available," Con said happily. He sat and toasted Harrison with an upraised glass. "The commodities markets, old son, that's the ticket."

"Really?" Harrison was not particularly interested but he wanted to be polite about Conrad's happiness.

"Absolutely," Con said. "Hell, Harrison, you're one of the few men in this town, no, by God, you're prob'ly the *only* man in town bright enough to understand the markets." He waggled his free hand in the air. "Most of them, the only thing they know is what the cattle buyers tell them."

"That's the truth," Harrison agreed.

"You, you understand intangibles. Most fellows aren't able to do that."

Harrison took a drink, but the glow he felt had little to do with the liquor.

"You and I, Harrison, we're a cut above the common run. We understand such things."

Harrison took another drink and nodded gravely. "We are," he said.

"That's exactly why I was so delighted to see you this afternoon," Con said. He leaned closer and lowered his voice. "I just got word in today's mail, Harrison. From my broker. I don't deal locally, you understand. I have a man in Kansas City." Burton smiled. "My last commodities investment, Harrison. Very sound. My broker put me onto it, although of course I checked it out myself. It came in at a profit of nearly three thousand. That's profit, mind, beyond my initial investment."

Harrison's eyes widened slightly, and he allowed a low whistle to escape his lips.

Three thousand dollars would be enough to take him to Kansas City and away from Redbluff. Even to New York. He envied Conrad that success.

"Grand, isn't it?"

"Truly," Harrison agreed.

"I knew you would appreciate the idea, Harrison. Not everyone here would. Investments. What do any of these fellows know about investments? Except the gentlemen in that corner over there, of course. And even they aren't having this kind of return. But then they aren't into commodities, not a one of them. Stocks, mostly, though Mr. Holton," Burton leaned closer, spoke more softly, "I know you won't breathe a word of this to anyone or I'd get into trouble with the bank."

"Not a word," Harrison said.

"Well, Mr. Holton, he invests in nothing but bonds. Not even stocks." He shook his head. "Small venture, small return is the way I see it. Mr. Holton hasn't the will to take the risks. More's the pity for our depositors is the way I see it."

Harrison nodded.

"I—" Burton stopped and sat upright for a moment, giving his friend a close look. He leaned back near Harrison's ear.

"I just now had a thought, Harrison. Would you be interested in a large return on your money? Say, a clear profit in the neighborhood of nine thousand? Maybe more, but I should think at least that much."

Harrison gaped at him. Nine thousand dollars would take a man anywhere he wanted to go, anywhere in the world, and take him in style.

"Think about it, Harrison. My broker has tipped me to another good investment. Of course I still must prove it out myself. Good as he is I wouldn't take even his word before I plunge. But it certainly sounds right." Burton paused long enough to take a drink, and Harrison gulped down a hearty jolt at the same time.

"If this is all that it sounds, Harrison, I stand to make in the neighborhood of eight thousand. But if I can take the whole block that is offered, why, I can increase that profit to nine thousand at the least."

He bent forward until he was whispering against Harrison's cheek. Harrison could feel his friend's breath on his skin and could smell the warm scent of whiskey in the air between them.

"You understand these things, Harrison, and I trust you to put a clamp on your tongue. If you were to come in with me for half of the deal, why, we could get a start on our fortunes right here." Con sat upright. His eyes were bright with excitement. "What do you think?"

"I . . . I'd have to think it over, Con."

"Of course. Of course, you would, Harrison. Hell, I have to check it out before we decide anything. Don't want to take unnecessary risks, you know. You don't have to tell me anything now, but I do want you to think about it." He grinned. "It could be a helluva deal for us, old friend. A helluva deal."

Harrison raised his glass toward Conrad and managed to smile, but within he was groaning.

How? he was asking himself. How could he ever find any money to invest? He had nothing, virtually nothing that was his own. Nothing, he thought bitterly, but a few articles of clothing and a place to sleep.

How would he ever find—how much did he need? He did not even know that. He asked.

"Four thosand," Con told him. "That's all it would take from each of us, Harrison. A mere four thousand apiece and we can more than double our money."

More than double, Harrison thought wistfully.

But four thousand dollars. There was no way. He might as well wish for clear title to the Kansas and Pacific Railroad. That would surely be as easy to come by. He sighed.

He was also unwilling to admit to Conrad that he could not raise that kind of money.

"I'll think about it," he said.

"Good. No, dammit, that's great. You think about it. Meantime, I'll check this thing out. Let me know in, oh, a week. Can you do that, Harrison? A week?"

"Sure, Conrad. I'll let you know in a week." He sighed again.

If only . . .

CHAPTER 23

"You are awfully pensive this evening," Bernard Cale said. Their dinner was over, the dishes washed and put away with the preacher's bachelor tidiness. Now they were sitting over coffee in the front room.

Harrison shrugged.

"Would you like a game?" Cale motioned toward the chessboard always ready on its small tilt-top table.

Harrison shook his head. "Not tonight if you don't mind."

"I don't mind." He paused. "Is it anything you would like to talk about?" A smile softened his expression. "The Romans have a very good idea in the confessional, you know.

"I . . ." Harrison did not particularly want to discuss the hopes and the dilemma that Conrad Burton had raised in him. "It is Uncle Stewart," he substituted. "I'm worried about him."

"Tell me about it."

Harrison gave his friend another shrug and told him about Albert coming back after so long, with no sign of Stewart but with his rope. The more he talked the more alarmed Harrison convinced himself he should be.

"It isn't like him to lose a rope that way," he said. "I'm afraid something has happened to him. Something dreadful, perhaps." He was beginning to believe it now. "I am afraid he has been killed. Alone out there. Riding after men who are known to steal. A thief would kill to protect himself, wouldn't he. Wouldn't he?"

"Possibly," Bernard said, "but not likely. It would be difficult to take a human life."

"Not here. Not these people," Harrison said. "They

have done it before, these people. My own uncle would kill another man over a few stolen beeves. They all would. And have. Just a few years ago they did it all the time.''

Cale laughed, shortly and without humor. ''Not so many of them as you seem to think, Harrison. Not many of them at all, even when the times were extreme. And things have certainly changed since then. I think you are exaggerating that. And I think your fears about Stewart may be equally unfounded. After all, you admit yourself that he is the kind of man who would stay on a trail long after reason suggests he should quit it. A lost rope is hardly reason to assume dire consequences. Think about that.''

Agitated now about Stewart's possible fate as well as Conrad Burton's unexpected opportunity, Harrison left his chair and began to pace the small room, his carefully nurtured limp forgotten for the moment.

Bernard sighed and picked up *The Life of Calvin,* which he was reading for perhaps the eighth time. Harrison would need time to work things out in the privacy of his own thoughts, he reasoned.

Harrison made several circuits of the room and stopped at the preacher's window, its curtains billowing lightly in the summer breeze.

It was nearly dark now and lamplight was showing in the windows of the town. A block away Harrison could see a wagon pull to a halt in front of the lesser of Redbluff's two saloons. It was a utility wagon, not a fancy driving rig but clean and freshly painted. Harrison's eyes narrowed when he saw Jesse Howard step down from the seat and tie the horses.

Harrison had not forgotten where and with whom Martha Trope spent her afternoon, and that knowledge added nothing to his mood.

Still, if Jesse was going into the saloon now, that meant that Martha had been returned to her home before nightfall. And it meant that the damned cowboy had not been invited to stay for supper.

Mrs. Trope would know the better catch for her pretty daughter, Harrison thought with some satisfaction. You could count on that. Martha would be better off with a gentleman of refinement and sensitivity than with a manure-smelling, sweaty cowboy like that damned Jesse Howard.

Even so, Harrison had less reason than ever to like Jesse.

He would have turned away from the window but another movement on the street caught his eye and a moment later he could hear the hoofbeats of loping horses and the cheerful, yipping catcalls of three riders.

Harrison's breath caught in his throat without his being aware of it. The three men were the three who said they were brothers from Texas. The three he had seen at the water hole with the bulls. Harrison's mouth was dry and involuntarily he shrank away from the window so that he was peering out from its edge rather than standing in front of it against the light from Bernard's reading lamp.

The brothers—if that was what they truly were, certainly they showed little or no family resemblance—waved and loudly greeted Jesse Howard and pulled their horses to a head-tossing halt beside his wagon.

It was too far away for Harrison to hear what was being said, but they all seemed cheerful enough. Quite friendly, in fact.

Jesse greeted them as if they were friends. The three Texans dismounted and tied their horses near Jesse's wagon, and the four of them went into the saloon together.

All the more reason to dislike and to distrust Jesse Howard, Harrison thought. The taste of bile was in his mouth and he thought fleetingly that if Howard were his own size . . . Harrison had never started a fight in his life but if he were ever going to do so, Jesse Howard would be his first choice.

And the Texans were as bad. Harrison shuddered. He did not *like* this country. Not the land; not the people.

All the more desperate reason to get away from here.

If only he could find the money to join Conrad Burton in that commodities venture he would be free. He would never have to look at the dreary, windswept grasslands of western Kansas again.

If only . . .

CHAPTER 24

Harrison walked gloomily down the nearly darkened street. Lamplight shone from the windows of the saloons up ahead, from the freight office beyond and from the nearer cafe. Only about half of the homes in Redbluff still showed light at their windows.

Damned one-horse town, Harrison thought. People go to bed with the sun and get up with the chickens. In a real city there would be bright lights and activities. Theater and clubs and entertainments to meet every taste, at any time of day. Not here. Not in Redbluff. Here everyone was too tight to burn a little lamp oil and too ignorant to know why they should. Even Bernard Cale had adopted the habit of retiring early, at a time when a civilized person's day would only be beginning to be of interest. Harrison scowled into the gloom that was around him. There was at least as much gloom within him.

He became conscious of footsteps behind him, footsteps that increased their pace after a moment. For an instant Harrison felt a thrill of fear clutch at his throat. After all, those damned Texas brothers were in town. He had seen them himself.

"Harrison." Even though he was forewarned that there was someone behind him, he started, his shoulders involuntarily hunching forward at the sound. "Wait up."

He recognized the voice and was able to relax. "Yes, Con?" He stopped to wait for Burton to catch up with him.

"You seem to be everywhere I look today." Con was smiling. He took Harrison's elbow and shook it lightly. "Have you had supper?"

"I did."

"Then I'll buy you a wedge of pie and some coffee. You can sit with me while I eat, can't you?"

Harrison shrugged. The idea of conversation, having people around him, was infinitely better than the thought of a lonely drive back to an empty bed and no one to talk with but Nelda.

"Good," Con declared. He led Harrison into the cafe and chose a table near the front window where they could see out onto the street. The cafe was empty except for a pair of men: Asa Hooten, who ran the freight office in the next block; and his laborer Billy Ryal, who was dignified with the title of assistant freightmaster but who was nothing but a laborer regardless. Con gave both men a cheerful greeting; Harrison gave them a tight smile, and he had to force that. Ryal had beaten him up once when they were both boys, and Harrison had never forgotten or forgiven him for that.

"I almost gave up on you tonight," the cafe proprietor, Rick Rickarts, said, obviously speaking to Burton. He was already bringing a plate to the table without waiting to take Burton's order. He set it down, slopping some gravy onto the oilcloth that covered the flimsy table, and asked, "Anything else?"

Con ordered pie for Harrison, and Rickarts was back with it and coffee and a basket of biscuits within moments. Choices at the cafe, unnamed except for a sign out front that read Eats, were limited to whatever Rickarts had chosen to cook that day. At least the meals always provided generous portions of aged beef. Rickarts was as close as the town had to a butcher. Meat that did not sell over the counter at the back of the cafe eventually sold on its tables.

"Have you been thinking about what we discussed earlier?" Con asked as he began to attack the plate of meat and potatoes that had been put in front of him.

"About very little else," Harrison admitted. "But I have no idea where I might be able to find that kind of money, Con. I hate to say it, but it is so."

Con nodded and shoved a greasy-looking wad of gravy and fried potato into his mouth. He swallowed quickly. "Kind of thought that might be so. No offense, Harrison.

I'm just trying to put us into a position of doing each other a favor. You know that, don't you?"

"I know that."

"Good." He took another bite and swallowed it as quickly as the first. "Did a little thinkin' on it myself, you see."

Harrison's eyebrows lifted. If Conrad could think of a solution . . . "Go on," he prompted.

"Simple," Con said. "Your uncle."

"I don't believe would be interested in speculations," Harrison said.

"I never said he would." Con paused for another mouthful of his dinner. "No offense, Harrison, but I don't believe Stewart would understand about the commodities market. Not like you and I do anyway. No, what I was thinking, that place out there is part yours anyway. Surely you should be entitled to use some of the cash flow. I mean, it's not exactly a secret that the ranchers around here do pretty well by themselves. And you an' Stewart have one of the bigger operations. I don't know how much he has, of course. I wouldn't look into his accounts even if he did much banking with us, which he doesn't. But I know he shouldn't be hurt if you used some of your capital out of the outfit."

Harrison sighed. "I'm not a partner in the ranch."

"Your daddy was."

"That was a long time ago. My . . . my uncle never cared much for my mother. I don't know what happened exactly, after he died, but certainly I am not a partner in the ranch."

"That seems odd," Con said. "I would've thought you'd be half owner anyway. Your dad was."

Harrison shrugged.

"Seems hardly fair," Con observed. "Your daddy did at least half the work building the place, back in the beginning when times were the worst around here. You'd think he would have left something to his only son, wouldn't you?"

Again Harrison shrugged. Regardless of what he did or did not think about it, the fact was that he had no real position. Except that of a poor relation.

"You ought to discuss it with your uncle, anyway. As a short-term loan if not as an entitlement," Con said.

"He's away right now, and . . ." Harrison was reminded of the fears he had had about Stewart when he was talking with Bernard.

The more he thought about it, the more certain he was that some disaster had befallen Stewart Wilke. He told Con about his suspicions, leaving out only the fact that he increasingly was coming to believe that the purported Texas "brothers" might be responsible.

"Damn, Harrison. It sounds to me like you *should* be worried. Gone that long and no trace of him except for a rope, why, anything might have happened to him. Especially dealing with thieves like that. You can't tell what a desperate man might do. And Stewart would sure be outnumbered by them. A lone man couldn't possibly drive off that many beeves." Con used half of a biscuit to sop up the last of the gravy from his plate. He popped it into his mouth and chewed thoughtfully for a moment.

"You know . . ." he said. He stopped and shook his head. "No, I shouldn't go to mentioning anything like that. Not at a time when you're worried so about your uncle."

"What?" Harrison insisted.

"I was just remembering that talk we'd had a while back. You know. Saying how you were going to come into possession of the place someday anyhow. I mean, if anything *has* happened to Stewart, then you have a right to use whatever cash is on hand. And, now mind you I'm hoping as much as you are that your uncle is all right and these fears are entirely unjustified, but if anything has happened to him, why, it might be I could use my part of the investment profits to pay over to you as a down payment on the place. Assuming you'd want to sell, that is."

"I . . ." Harrison shook his head. "I don't know how to answer something like that, Con."

"Of course you don't. Hell, I'm sorry I brought it up. Look, with any luck at all your uncle and the hands will be riding back in tomorrow with those thieves in tow, and everything will be fine." He smiled. "For all we know, they could be home already, getting some sleep after all that riding and chasing. I'm sorry I said anything. Really.''

"It's okay. You were only trying to be helpful." He pushed his half-eaten piece of pie away—it was not very good pie—and stood. "I better be getting back out there. Thanks for the dessert. And for the help.''

"I'm glad I . . . well, I wouldn't want to cause you any distress. I hope you know that.''

"I do.'' They shook hands, and Harrison left the cafe.

He walked down the street more briskly this time and was not even upset when he passed the front of the saloon. Inside he could see Jesse Howard and the three Texans bellied up to the bar with glasses in their hands and laughter on their smug faces.

Harrison grimaced slightly as he passed but otherwise ignored the four of them.

If those Texans were responsible for his uncle coming to harm, he decided, they were going to pay for it. He would see to that. Somehow.

He reclaimed his rig, still parked in front of the mercantile, and headed for home at a brisk jog. All of a sudden he was anxious to learn if there had been any news about his uncle.

CHAPTER 25

Harrison was wandering aimlessly through the grove, his cold dinner concluded. Most of the families that had come in to church today were also finishing their meals, the men forming into small groups to talk and smoke while their women packed soiled dishes and leftover foods back into baskets. Before long someone would organize a ball game. Harrison was thinking about joining them this time. He had enjoyed his last experience with bat and ball.

He passed the scarred trunk of an ancient cottonwood and found himself unexpectedly face to face with Martha and Jesse Howard. They had been standing close together on the other side of the tree, and Harrison had not seen them there or he would have turned in another direction.

Jesse looked ill at ease in a suit and high collar. Harrison saw with some satisfaction that the sleeves of his coat were a shade too short for the length of his arms—it obviously was a suit purchased from a rack and not properly tailored to Howard's height.

Better yet, the tall cowboy looked angry. His jaw bulged and he seemed to be gritting his teeth.

Martha, on the other hand, looked very pretty with the blush of color in her cheeks. Her eyes were very bright. "Harrison," she exclaimed loudly, "I am so glad to see you." She turned to him and placed a hand inside his elbow.

He had come up just as they were having a disagreement, Harrison realized with satisfaction. Good. Jesse Howard was an insufferable ass. It was high time Martha realized it.

"You are very pretty today," Harrison said, glad that Jesse was there to overhear and to seethe in helpless frustration while Harrison paid the pretty girl a compliment.

"Thank you." Martha moved close against him and tipped her head back to flatter him with her attentions. "Would you mind walking with me, Harrison?" Pointedly she added, "I would enjoy some *civilized* company this afternoon."

"Of course," Harrison said gallantly. He turned Martha so that her back was to Jesse Howard and led her away with a feeling of triumphant pleasure. "Down by the stream, perhaps?"

"That would be very nice, Harrison," she agreed.

With Jesse behind and ignored, if not forgotten, Harrison led the girl away from the people in the grove to the streambank a short stroll away. He felt very good being seen with the prettiest girl in town on his arm. He led her to a sloping, fallen log and watched with pleasure while she fluffed her skirts wide and sat on the use-polished wood. Harrison took the liberty of sitting beside her.

"Are you all right, Martha?"

She shrugged. "I am now, thanks to you."

"I hope . . ." He did not know quite how to finish. It would have been boorish and, worse, probably would have had quite the opposite effect from what he desired if he made any direct attack on Jesse Howard at this point. He left the thought unspoken.

"What about you, Harrison?"

"Oh, I'm quite recovered from my accident now. But I am worried about Uncle Stewart." Martha's eyes were wide and soft with sympathy, prompting him to go on. "It has been so long, and now Tim and Al seem to have disappeared also. Aunt Nelda is trying not to show it, but she is beside herself with worry." Harrison sighed dramatically. "I am convinced that somet ng dreadful has happened. Otherwise we surely would have heard something by now."

Martha replaced her hand on his arm, and the warmth

from her fingers was maddeningly pervasive. He could feel very little else.

Her cheeks were still slightly flushed and her eyes were very bright. She tossed her head to sweep back a strand of hair that had escaped its pins, and Harrison thought she had never looked prettier. She leaned closer so that he could feel the heat of her body on his arm from shoulder to elbow, and his breath caught in his throat.

"Harrison, would you . . . would you think it terribly forward of me . . . I mean, would you think me a hussy if I asked you to hold me?"

He could scarcely believe what he had heard. He swallowed hard and, still unable to accept his good fortune, moved his arm around behind her. Martha melted into the curl of his arm, and Harrison was painfully aware of the contact with her body. The heat he could feel in his cheeks told him that he was blushing, and he fought to conquer it.

He turned his face to look at her and found her lips only inches from his. It seemed only natural to kiss her.

The touch of her lips was dizzying. The blood rushed to his head and pounded in his ears, and he was hoping desperately that his breath was untainted from his dinner. His free hand went to her slim waist, and he was acutely conscious of the feel of her flesh separated from his by so little cloth. His dizziness became worse, and he braced himself, suddenly terrified that he might lose his balance and topple with her from their perch on the old log.

Martha drew her head back slightly, breaking the light touch of their lips, and Harrison opened his eyes. He did not remember having closed them, but then he was having difficulty accepting the reality of any of this. Her eyes, so close to his, were wide open, and he got the impression she had kept her eyes open throughout the kiss. Harrison wondered briefly if that was normal. He had practically no prior experience to judge from.

Martha smiled at him gently. "Now you must surely think me a hussy," she said.

"No, oh no, I . . ." he stammered. "Not at all, I . . .

I think you are the most wonderful, the kindest, the most lovely—"

"Shhhh." She reached up and laid a finger lightly across his lips. She smiled again, almost sadly he thought although surely he must have been mistaken about that after the marvelous thing that had just happened, and said, "You are a nice man, Harrison Wilke."

Harrison's heart was pounding wildly. He took a firmer grip on her and pulled her to him, bending his lips toward her again.

Martha's body stiffened slightly and she arched her head back, withdrawing just out of reach. "No, please."

It took all of his self-control to stop, to release his hold on her. He was puzzled but accepted her right to decide. At least, he realized, she relaxed immediately, her body soft and pliant again under his touch. He still had his arm around her and his other hand remained at her waist.

"I'm sorry," she whispered.

"The fault was mine," Harrison said. "I understand."

She smiled. Easily and with genuine warmth this time, and leaned against his shoulder within the protective curl of his arm.

Of course he understood, Harrison told himself. A girl of any quality, and certainly Martha was a young lady of the highest quality, could not allow herself untoward license at such an early stage of courtship. It was enough, it was soaringly, impossibly, marvelously more than enough, that she had so openly declared her acceptance of his intentions already. To have asked for more now would have been to demean her, and that he would never do. Never, he told himself sternly.

"Could we walk back now, Harrison?"

"Of course. Anything you wish, Martha." He smiled. "Anything."

They walked back slowly to the gathering in the grove, and Harrison was careful to keep a discreet distance between them. It would not do to place their understanding on public display. A courtship must be undertaken properly, with decent intervals for the affections to grow and the correct amenities to be observed. There would be plans to make, formal discussions to take place between himself and Mr. Trope, so many things to arrange, so much to be decided.

Harrison's heart was filled almost to the point of bursting, and he felt that he was barely in contact with the earth as he walked with Martha at his side.

He thought about telling her some of the things that he was feeling, but already they were too close to the others and it would not have done, not at all, for anyone else to overhear. Harrison Wilke was happier at that moment than at any previous time in his existence.

CHAPTER 26

Harrison could not sleep that night. The harder he tried to shove thoughts of Martha out of his mind, the more persistent she was in lingering there. It was as if her presence was a tangible thing, there with him in the silence of his small bedroom. Every small, daylight contact with her remained with him in the night, each sensitive point of contact burning as if she had branded him with her slightest touch. He could still feel that brief touch of her lips on his, could recall with absolute precision the contours of her back and waist. The memory was almost as remarkable as the reality had been.

He lay wide-eyed in the darkness, conscious of every wisp of moving air that came through his open window, aware of every footfall as the horses shifted back and forth in the distant corral beyond that window. His senses seemed to have been elevated to a new and unheard-of pitch. Every sensation was raised to a new level of awareness. He could feel the weight of the sheet against his chest. He could hear the pulse of his heartbeat in his ears. He was, he concluded happily, very much in love with the girl who was the prize catch of Redbluff and probably of all of Kansas.

But there was so *much* to plan for.

The courtship, he thought, should proceed at a pace that would be comfortable for Martha. A year or even longer.

Then the ritual proposal to be placed before her father for his formal consent.

What if he would not give it? Harrison thought with sudden alarm.

Nonsense, he chided himself. Martha would pave the

way for that long before the actual occurrence. And he was certain that Mrs. Trope would be a champion for his suit. Mrs. Trope had better hopes for her only daughter than marriage to some rank, randy cowhand. She knew what she had in Martha; she would want the girl to link her life with that of a man who was cultured and sensitive. Definitely not with the likes of Jesse Howard.

Harrison grinned into the night. Not that he had to worry about Jesse now. Not again. Not *ever* again. With Martha Trope at his side, he had bested that son of a bitch once and for all time.

There was still much to be concerned about, though.

The marriage should take place within a year and a half. Within two years at the very longest. Harrison groaned and wondered if he could wait so long to claim Martha as his own. He would have to. He could not possibly dishonor her by abusing her the way some damned cowboy would treat a common trollop.

In the meantime there would be much to do. But afterward Harrison would have to take charge and accept responsibility for Martha's future well-being.

That would be difficult, he knew.

With a sense of horror he realized that then he would have to provide a home and a livelihood, not just for himself but for her as well.

The prospects for accomplishing that here in Redbluff were depressingly dim. The choices were so few. He could build a house here at the ranch he loathed and turn lovely Martha into an overworked, quickly overaged duplicate of his aunt. Or he could clerk in Leon Trope's mercantile.

Neither prospect was appealing in the slightest.

On the Running W he would be sentencing both himself and Martha to eternal crudity.

In the store he would only be exchanging sleeve garters for chaps. That too would inevitably be a dead and dreary end to all the hopes and the dreams Harrison harbored, dreams of bright lights and gay companions and a dignified way of life.

There *had* to be some better way, some alternate path that would allow him to express his caring for Martha with tangible proofs in the form of a good life. A fine home. Elegant clothing. Civilized entertainments.

He shook his head.

For a person who had nothing—except for deep yearnings—the task that lay before him seemed insurmountable.

To give Martha all that he desired, desired for *both* of them, he would have to take her away from Redbluff and from everything it represented.

They would have to go East. To Kansas City or St. Louis. To Chicago. Better yet, to New York or Boston. Only there would a young man of Harrison's vision and breeding be able to realize the full scope of his hopeful prospects.

But that would take capital. They would need capital to locate and to live on while Harrison secured a position that would be worthy of his sensitivity and his capabilities.

He had no capital. He had nothing to build on and little time to assemble a start on their fortunes.

Conrad Burton offered the only scant hope Harrison had or hoped to have, and his venture would require investment capital to begin with.

Harrison sighed. A family could be sustained on six hundred dollars per year. A decent home could be obtained for two thousand dollars or so. Even in the cities? he asked himself. He was not sure. Even more than that might be required in the East. He had no way of knowing.

The figure $9,000 kept roaring through his mind. That was what Con had said their shared commodities investment could return.

With nine thousand dollars in ready cash, a man could provide his bride with a small but quite elegant home. Give her a wardrobe of fashionable garments. Buy a membership in a good club and perhaps a literary society. Purchase a theater box. And still have money left over, enough to provide the basic needs for several years while appropriate employment was found.

Better yet, Harrison thought, with that much capital a man could become an investor.

Buy low and sell dear, that was the key to success. It was a simple concept but apparently grasped only by the few. Harrison had the vision to grasp, no to embrace, that concept. He would do well in business. He knew that with absolute certainty. He had no doubt at all that with nine thousand dollars in capital he would be equipped to make his way in the world and to provide truly well for Martha besides.

All he needed was a chance.

Misery descended on him in the gloom of his darkened room. He had as much chance of achieving that start as those cattle thieves had of escaping with a tonguelashing if or when Stewart Wilke caught up with them.

Unless, as Harrison already more than half suspected, Stewart already had caught up with them. Unless Stewart was dead and gone now. Then things might be different.

Harrison had no fondness for Stewart, but even so he felt a thrill of distaste to realize that Stewart's disappearance could well be Harrison's only chance at the achievement of his life's goals.

He felt distaste. And excitement too. He disliked admitting that, even to himself. Yet it was undeniable. With Stewart gone, as more and more it seemed that he must be, a door was opened to Harrison's future.

And to Martha's future happiness and well-being as well.

Stewart was dead. He really must be. He had been gone for a month now. If he were still alive he surely would have been able to send word back to Nelda long before now, yet he had not done so. Stewart had not been heard of since Harrison's accident, when Harrison and Tim turned back from the chase to hurry Harrison to Redbluff and medical attention.

The man had been alone on the plains, alone with a gun and the uncertainties of half-wild range horses and with a gang of cattle thieves in front of him. Anything might have happened to him in the time since he was last seen. Anything at all. And surely he would have sent word to Nelda if he were still alive.

Tim and Al did not really enter the equation, Harrison realized. They were as dull and plodding as the rest of their breed, and they had been taught to follow Stewart

Wilke's lead in all things. If they set out to find Stewart they could not be expected to return until they found Stewart or discovered his body. And in the emptiness of the plains, that search could be a long one indeed.

In the meantime, Harrison realized, there was a possibility lying before him, the potential for his entire future, locked into Con Burton's offer to enter a partnership with the only other person of vision in all of Redbluff, Harrison Wilke.

And with Stewart Wilke gone, and almost certainly dead, there was not even any chance to plead with his uncle for the loan of the four thousand dollars he needed to enter the partnership.

Son of a bitch, he cursed silently to himself, over and over again in the darkness of his lonely bedroom.

CHAPTER 27

"She isn't here," Mr. Trope snapped. He turned angrily away and bent again to resume poring over his accounts receivable ledger with Mrs. Brighton.

In spite of Harrison having been grumped at by Martha's father he was barely able to restrain a smile that was trying to tickle the corners of his mouth. The reason for Leon Trope's displeasure was obvious and did not really involve Harrison. Luella Brighton was often as confused as she was stubborn, and trying to make her understand a problem with her account would be frustrating indeed. Harrison decided he could inquire further about Martha's whereabouts at another, better time. He collected his mail from the counter where Trope had slammed it and left the store.

He sighed when he reached the boardwalk. He had planned his evening around a visit with Martha, and now she did not seem to be available.

Worse, he could not even go visit with Bernard Cale. Coming into town on a Wednesday evening had been part of his plan. Bernard would be holding midweek prayer meeting tonight, and Harrison had fully intended to invite Martha out on the pretext of going to the meeting. He had not really intended to arrive at the church, though.

Damnation, he told himself.

He brightened. It was certainly early for Martha and her mother to be thinking in terms of trousseau and hope chest. But not impossibly so in light of the understanding that was now between them. It was at least possible that the two women could have gone to Trentsville for a day or two to accomplish some of the shopping that would not be available in Redbluff.

Harrison was not entirely sure that the Tropes could not order everything they needed through their store suppliers, but it seemed at least a possibility. Under the circumstances he decided to regard Martha's absence as a good sign.

He filled his lungs deeply with the clean plains air, coughed a little from the dust raised by the passage of a freight wagon on the street and managed to feel expansive in spite of that.

With so much daylight remaining, the merchants up and down the short street would be open for business for several hours more, but across the way the employees were leaving the Redbluff Bank of Commerce. Charles Holton locked and rattled the door behind them.

Conrad Burton was with them. He smiled and waved across the street toward Harrison, turned to say something to his coworkers and stepped down into the street to cross toward his friend.

So be it, Harrison thought. He was not yet ready to give Con any answer about his generous proposal, but he could visit with him. At the very least he could do that.

"Howdy, old son," Con said cheerfully. He was grinning to give the lie to the crude form of speech he had to employ day in and day out in his dealings with the people of Redbluff.

Harrison wished briefly that he could be more like Con, fitting in with these people even though he was superior to them. Conrad clapped him on the shoulder and turned him deftly down the street.

"Got plans for the evening? No? Come along with me then. It's too early to eat, so we'll stop and have a drink first, all right?" He was not really asking questions, as he was already directing Harrison in the direction Con intended to take him. Harrison allowed himself to be guided without protest.

To Harrison's surprise Con took him past the entrance to the better of Redbluff's saloons and continued on toward the edge of town, toward the cruder place where the cowhands and teamsters did their drinking.

"No sense in having Mr. Holton overhear," Con said easily. "Not that I need his approval for my ventures, but it wouldn't do for anyone who might understand to hear about this deal, would it? Course not."

"I'm not really—" Harrison began to protest, but Con cut him short.

"I know, but it will be all right in here. These good ol' boys think commodities are foods you can stuff in a saddlebag. No harm done even if they do hear us talk."

"But I—"

"It's all *right*, I tell you. Come on now."

Before Harrison could say anything more he was seated at one of the rickety tables in the saloon, and Con was at the bar ordering a pair of mugs for them.

Harrison looked around nervously. As long as he had been in Redbluff, and as long as this run-down saloon had been here, he had never stepped foot inside the place before. It had a reputation for being rowdy and boisterous.

He was not sure what he expected. Something short of horns and tails on the patrons, but not very far short of it at that. Loud talk and drunkenness and painted women at the very least. What he saw was a perfectly ordinary sawdust floor, customers quietly drinking and not a female, painted or otherwise, anywhere in sight. There was the usual free lunch spread out on the end of the bar. As far as Harrison could tell, the only difference between this place and the more socially accepted saloon closer to the center of the business district was that here there was no mirror behind the bar and the glassware was all made of nonbreakable tin. The quiet atmosphere was almost a disappointment, and if there was any sin or lewdness going on here it was being done out of sight. Harrison sat stiffly in his chair and waited for Con's return.

"There you go, old hoss." Con set a mug of beer in front of Harrison, sat and took a deep draught from his own mug. "That sure tastes good after a dry day." He licked a thin foam of suds from his upper lip and leaned back in his chair. "Good to see you again so soon, Harrison, I swear it is."

Harrison smiled at him and tasted the beer. It was neither better nor worse than the slightly sour brew served up the street. Beer was a taste Harrison had never acquired. He tried another swallow.

"Go on," Con urged. "Drink up. We have more celebrating to do."

Harrison drank, as instructed. "Now what are we celebrating?"

Con grinned and leaned forward across the table to put his lips closer to Harrison's ear. "Heard from my broker again. Yesterday, it was. I'm so damned excited I'd have been out to see you this weekend if you hadn't come in on your own."

"Really?" Harrison took another drink.

"You bet. I'd asked him for more information about this little venture of ours, and of course I've been doing some investigating on my own. It all checks out, Harrison, exactly the way he said it would."

That would make it all the harder for him to tell Conrad that he simply did not have the capital necessary to join the partnership. Harrison took another long swallow and was surprised to discover that he had come to the end of his mug.

"Here, let me refill that for you." Con was up and gone before Harrison could protest.

When he came back Conrad launched into a voluble, highly animated account of their expected profits. Harrison sat politely and listened, unwilling to disturb his friend's mood by admitting that at least as far as Harrison was concerned the deal was off.

Con paused long enough to bring them each another refill and then resumed his happy discussion.

Harrison was barely listening to him at that point. Thoughts of Martha kept running through his mind. Thoughts about her placing her trust in him. Thoughts about the uncertainty of their future together until or unless he could find a proper way to support her. She deserved so much, and he was prepared to give so little. Harrison sighed. Conrad brought them another round.

Funny thing, Harrison observed. The beer in this place was actually quite a bit better than that served up the street. It really was not bad at all here.

He grinned across the table at his friend, happy to be here with Con, and was mildly amused to discover that his ears felt a bit numb whenever his jaw moved. He waggled his jaw a little to test that discovery, then reached up to pinch his earlobe. Sure enough, he had been right. The tip of his nose tingled slightly too. He decided that was quite funny indeed.

"Have another, Harrison. Here." Con was back at the table before Harrison realized he had left it. "By damn, boy, we do have a lot to be glad about, don't we?"

"Sure as hell do," Harrison agreed. He was beginning to feel quite as cheerful as Conrad. He took a long swallow from the freshly refilled mug.

"If it's all right with you," Con was saying, "I intend to wire my broker tomorrow committing us for the entire block."

Harrison nodded and blinked owlishly across the vast distance that was the tabletop. He took another swallow from the mug. Damn thing was empty again. No, Con was back and it was full again. That was much better.

"That will give us a week to cover the purchase. Since I already have an account with him, we can go ahead and commit now and cover the buy through the mail. Soon as you get your share to me I'll send him a postal money order. I think that will be better, everything considered, than getting a bank draft through Mr. Holton, don't you agree?"

Con's voice sounded faint and rather distant, as if he were speaking through a tin tube. Harrison took another drink. "You know what's best." His own voice had a thin, metallic echo too. That was even funnier than the way Con sounded. Harrison began to giggle.

"Are you all right?" Con's face was immediately beside Harrison's. He looked concerned.

"Damn right I'm all right," Harrison informed him, pronouncing his words with careful precision. He grinned. "How about another beer?"

Con relaxed and smiled. "Harrison old friend, I would say that we are entitled to one. Maybe even several more. After all, we have a lot to celebrate tonight."

CHAPTER 28

Harrison's lips felt numb and his cheeks fuzzy. Fuzzy? He pondered whether that would be accurate, decided he did not particularly care. Numb, fuzzy, what was the difference? He had a friend and a girl friend and bright prospects for the future. What more could a man want? He felt good. He felt *damn* good.

"B'God, Conrad, it's my turn to buy."

"Aw, that's all right. I know your uncle doesn't give you much spending money."

"No, now, I got . . . I got . . ." He reached into his pocket and pulled out some coins. He had a little trouble seeing what they were and had to hold them close under his eyes to make them out. "I got more'n a dollar here. My turn to buy."

"Whatever you say, Harrison." Con grinned. "Partner," he corrected.

"Partner. Damn straight, partner. That's us, right? Right." Harrison slid his chair back from the table and stood. He had to be very careful to lock his knees to keep from slumping back into that darn chair. His lips felt very dry. He licked them and then did it again because he was not sure he could feel it when he did so.

He moved toward the bar at a stiff-legged, slow gait, using great care to keep his balance. It would not do for anyone to think he had become tipsy. No dignity in that. It would not do. He felt like he was walking on stilts. He could remember as a kid using lengths of forked branches as short stilts. He remembered that very well. Felt very much the same. Sure. He had done it then, he could do it now. No problem. One foot at a time. Slowly now. Keep the back straight and the chin up. Wouldn't do for anyone to think he was tiddly. Nossir, that would not do. He grinned at his own success. There wasn't a one of them could guess that he felt fuzzy. Nossir, not a one of them.

He stopped at least a pace short of the bar, reached out to lean on it for support and missed. He lurched forward, lost his balance for a moment and came up short with his ribs slamming into the edge of the bar. He recoiled, reeled sideways and caught himself against a man standing there.

"What're you doing?" Harrison demanded of the impertinent fellow. Cheeky person, getting in his way like that.

"Howdy," the man said cheerfully. He pushed Harrison upright with one hand and raised a mug of beer to toast him with the other.

Harrison blinked and brought the fellow's face into focus. Lord Almighty, he thought with sudden alarm. "You're one of them . . . one of *those*," he corrected, "Texans."

"That's right," the man agreed. He turned his head away. "Barkeep, I think the little fella here wants another round."

Harrison blinked and reached out for the edge of the bar for support. His ribs still hurt. *"Little?"* he barked.

The Texan—tall, handsome son of a bitch, just like that miserable Jesse Howard; they were all alike, these horse-smelling cowboys, Harrison thought—smiled at him. "No offense," he said.

"I assure you, sir, that I take offense at your depre . . . dep . . . derogatory reference," Harrison declared. He was proud that his enunciation was perfect.

"None intended," the Texan said mildly.

"You should be more careful in reference to your betters," Harrison informed him. He wrinkled his nose and blinked several times. "You smell of cow manure, sir. Please stand away." He pointed down the bar limply.

"I reckon," the Texan said, "you should put a cork in it, little fella, 'fore you make somebody mad here. An' that somebody just might could be me." He no longer sounded nearly so mild as he had before.

"Move aside, sir," Harrison ordered. He waved the Texan down the bar again. The motion upset his balance and again he lurched into the man.

"Dammit, I—"

"It's all right," another voice said soothingly. "Don't worry 'bout it, Tom. That's just ol' Harrison. We kinda make allowances for him around here." The voice chuckled. "Hell, we ain't ever seen him drunk before. Maybe it's a good sign. Though of what I couldn't exactly tell you. But leave him be. He doesn't mean any harm, an' he's never acted human before."

Harrison was reasonably sure that he had just been insulted. He leaned forward around the bulk of the Texan to see who was talking about him like that.

He should have known. It was that damned Jesse Howard. In the flesh. He should have known that the likes of Howard would be chummy with those cow-stealing Texans. Birds of a feather and all that. Huh! He wondered where that damned bartender was with his and Con's beers. A gentleman did not have to stand here and accept insults from the likes of these people. Harrison banged his fist on the bar.

"See?" Jesse said. Apropos of what, Harrison could not quite decide.

The barman came with a pair of freshly filled mugs, and Harrison fumbled his money onto the bar. He laid it all down, as that was considerably easier than trying to sort out the correct amount. Whatever that was.

"Here, I'll carry these for you."

"I can manage quite well for myself and—"

"Dammit, Harrison, you couldn't walk half a step with your hands full. Tom, fetch your little friend along, an' I'll take these to his table."

Harrison felt himself being lifted and guided. It only lasted for a moment, then he was in his chair again and Con was leaning close and saying something to him but he could not make out what it was his friend was saying.

Not that it mattered. At least that damned Texan and that damned Jesse Howard were no longer around. He craned his head to look, and he was perfectly right about that. They were at the bar, drinking. Soaking up alcohol.

That was probably befitting someone of their class. Drinking and carousing. That was all their kind was good for. Persons of class need not associate with that type.

Harrison raised his mug and toasted Conrad. He took a deep drink of the fine-tasting beer.

He sighed. Everything was going to be just fine. He had shown that damned Jesse Howard, hadn't he. Jesse Howard had his low-life friends, but Harrison Wilke had the affections of Martha Trope. That was showing him. Harrison took another drink.

He had to admit one thing. They served good beer here. The best.

He grinned across the table at Con.

CHAPTER 29

Harrison remembered every moment of it. Worse than the ache that was trying to sledgehammer its way out of his skull, worse than the dryness of his mouth and the greasy queasiness in his stomach, worst of all was the fact that he could remember each and every unlovely bit of what had happened the night before.

He could not remember a thing about the ride home nor what, if anything, he had had for supper. If he absolutely *had* to lose a portion of his memory why could it not have been that despicable period in the damned saloon.

He was not that fortunate. The incidents in the saloon he could remember almost word for word and drink for drink. He shuddered.

It was bad enough that he had committed himself as Conrad Burton's investment partner—and why he had done *that* he could not now begin to imagine—but, dammit all, he had had to suffer the humiliation of Jesse Howard's assistance and that manure-smelling Texan's amusement. *That* was the worst, the unforgivable part of it.

He shook his head, feeling as if his brains had expanded and were about to burst out of their confinement, and felt infinitely sorry for himself.

Not only had he forced himself into a position now of owing Conrad Burton four thousand dollars in almost instant cash, but he had been made light of by a man who—as Harrison had seen with his own eyes—was a cattle thief. And with that damned Jesse Howard there beside him as witness and abettor.

Harrison sat up in his narrow bed and discovered he

was still dressed. He stank and did not even *want* to know of what.

Maybe some of what he had done could still be corrected, he thought. He pulled himself upright and for the first time gained some idea of what it must be like to be old and enfeebled. He was still decidedly shaky when he went out and, making liberal use of the banister for support, made his way downstairs.

Aunt Nelda seemed to be nowhere around, which was probably just as well. He checked the big clock in the parlor and shuddered again. It was the middle of the afternoon. By now Con would have long since dispatched his telegraph message telling the stockbroker that Conrad Burton and Harrison Wilke were committed to the purchase of a block of—

Of what? The realization came hard that Harrison did not even know what commodity it was that Con had committed them to. Money that was not even his had been duly invested. And he did not know in what.

Harrison groaned. He gave some fond thought to the prospect that he might die of his continuing misery. Ideally sometime within the next few minutes.

When that did not come to pass he walked weakly into the kitchen. There were some leftover biscuits in a tin plate on the side of the range, but the very thought of food was nearly enough itself to send him into the dry heaves. He had some dim recollection of stopping along the way during the night to lose whatever it was Con had fed him for supper and of trying to lose still more long after the available supply was exhausted.

There was coffee on the range too, and he poured himself some. Sipped at it and was pleased when his stomach accepted the awful stuff.

A bath was what he needed next, he decided. He seriously doubted that he could manage to heat water for himself, but at least he could sluice off some of the smell that hung in the air wherever he turned. He thought about going back upstairs and rejected the idea; that would be asking just too, too much.

He tottered out the back door in search of cleansing

water, hoping that wherever his aunt had gotten to it
was far from the ranch yard.

"Come in, Con." Harrison stepped aside and let his
friend through the door. It was Saturday morning, and
he had more than half expected Con's visit.

Con removed his hat and hung it on the antler rack by
the front door. He grinned. "You look somewhat better
than the last time I saw you."

Harrison grunted.

"I kind of expected you in town before now, but I
guess you've been busy out here with Stewart gone and
everything."

Harrison nodded. That, at least, was the literal truth.
He had never been so busy around the damned ranch
before. Working off the guilts was what he had been
doing. Nelda must have seen—or at least smelled—his
condition Wednesday night, but she had not mentioned
it. Nor had she mentioned the way Harrison immersed
himself in work afterward. The horses had never been
so well tended, hinges so well oiled, posts so stoutly
strapped. He had even repainted the family wagon gleam-
ing maroon on the sideboards and a brilliant yellow for
the spokes. At least when he took Martha for a drive,
which he fully intended after church, she would not
have to be ashamed of the vehicle.

That was small consolation.

And at least he felt physically recovered now.

"You do have the—"

Harrison cut him short with a finger pressed to his
lips. "Just a minute." He went back to the kitchen
doorway and poked his head through it. "Con Burton is
here," he told his aunt. "We're going to use Uncle
Stewart's office if you don't mind."

She smiled. "Go right ahead." Her smile was not
very convincing. After so long the strain of wondering
and worrying about her husband was beginning to tell on
her.

"Thanks." Harrison went back to the foyer. "This
way." He led Con into the dark, paneled room that was
his uncle's private preserve and closed the door behind

them. He knew from long experience that anything said in there would not be overheard elsewhere in the house.

"I hope you have the cash on hand, Harrison," Con said without preamble, "because I have to have it in the mail Monday morning early as possible. The postmark might be enough, but I don't want to count on that, you know."

Harrison nodded unhappily. Over the past few days he had become resigned to the inevitable.

He had said he would do it. Now he had no choice. If he welshed on his agreement now it would not only remove him from the venture, it would discredit Conrad as well. Con could not cover the entire block by himself. That was why he had invited Harrison into the partnership to begin with.

Besides, Harrison kept telling himself, this seeming error could well be the greatest of blessings in disguise. Timidity would have forced him to reject Con's offer if he had been acting logically. But as it was, forced into the partnership, it could only result in a bright future for himself and for Martha.

It was all a matter of fate, Harrison had decided.

He was being given opportunity in spite of himself. It was a gift of sorts, and now it was up to him to grasp the opportunity and make use of it.

"I have the money right here," he said.

Con nodded and seemed to relax.

With no hesitation—he had thought about this over and over during the past several days and had long since reached his conclusions—Harrison went to Stewart's desk.

The key to his uncle's lockbox was kept in the bottom right drawer. Harrison had seen Stewart use it often enough.

Harrison had not been able to convince himself that Stewart would have loaned him the money had the old bastard been at home—that would have been going too far—but he was more and more convinced of two things. One was that Stewart by now must surely have met with misfortune, either from the outlaws he was chasing or from accident on the uncertain and always dangerous plains. If that were so, then this money would be Harrison's by right if not exactly by formal execution of a will. The other was that no harm was being done even if Stewart was alive and well and merely delayed. As soon as the investment paid off, Harrison would be able to replace the borrowed money. He would keep for himself only that amount that was profit. It was all quite simple, he had decided.

He got the key from its "hiding" spot underneath Stewart's stock ledger and went to the massive chest where Stewart kept an assortment of worn-out gloves and gauntlets and belts and other such useless stuff. The man seemed incapable of throwing such things away. The lockbox was at the bottom of the jumble of articles. Harrison shoveled them aside and opened the box.

The only question—and it was one that had been haunting him—was how much cash Stewart chose to keep there. It was something he had never wondered about before and something he had been afraid to check for himself until now.

He held the lid aside and breathed a sigh of some relief. The orderly rows of dull yellow coin would be more than enough to meet the four-thousand-dollar obligation.

Not a great deal more than enough, but sufficient, in any event.

With Stewart gone, possibly forever, he would never know about the loan. There seemed no reason for him to tell Nelda about it either.

Harrison reached into the box and began to count the money out into his friend's hand.

CHAPTER 30

It was bad enough having to sit still during Bernard Cale's normally enjoyable services while there was so much on his mind. Optimism about the future he and Martha would share, nervousness about the money he had given Conrad, fear that his uncle would return too soon and, oddly, another fear that he would not return at all. Now that Harrison had chosen to go his own way, and had taken the money from Stewart's lockbox to finance his future, he found himself genuinely concerned about his uncle's welfare for the first time.

All of that was weighing on his thoughts and making the sense of Bernard's message escape him entirely.

But the worst part was that he was unable to sit with Martha and her family.

It was his own fault. Nighttime fretfulness had kept him tossing in a tangle of sheets far into the morning hours. As a consequence he overslept and only just barely reached the church before the doors were swung shut, signaling the last seating for latecomers. Now Harrison had to sit wedged into a back pew between the Hanson children and Melinda Kreger. The children were fidgety, and Miss Kreger needed a bath. Harrison could remember more enjoyable Sunday services.

Bernard's voice droned on with whatever it was he was saying, while toward the front of the small church Martha sat with her family in their accustomed spot. From where he was all Harrison could see of her was the glossy sheen of hair on the back of her head.

Still, the freshly painted wagon waited outside. And if he had not had time to pack the picnic lunch he had intended there would be time enough later to correct

118

that. If necessary he could borrow a dollar from Bernard or perhaps from Conrad and have a box dinner made up for them at the cafe. He thought about that during the final hymn, not joining in so intense was his concentration, and decided that would be the best course of action.

He was anxious to get Martha away from the other families that would be gathered in the grove so he could tell her about his news. About *their* prospects.

The final hymn ended and Bernard swept down the center aisle to be at the door for the obligatory handshaking afterward.

When the congregation stood and the people began to file slowly out, Harrison became angry. That damned Jesse Howard had shown up. From his seat in the back of the sanctuary Harrison had not been able to see him before, but the cowboy had been sitting in the same pew with the Tropes. Almost as bad, he had had the gall to drag the three Texans with him.

The Texans were not even dressed fit to be seen in public, much less in a church. As at the dance, they wore no ties and two of them actually came to church in vests and shirt sleeves. Harrison glared at them, his courage rising in these surroundings, but none of them seemed to notice him.

Philistines, Harrison accused silently.

The Tropes and Jesse Howard and the insufferable Texans—cattle thieves, Harrison was positive—drifted out with the others while Harrison hung back so he could have a private word with Bernard and borrow the needed dollar. The wait was interminably long.

"Do you have a minute, Bernard?" he was able to ask finally.

Cale smiled. "Of course, Harrison." He waved a good-bye to the last of the congregation and greeted Harrison warmly. "Was there something in particular?"

"As a matter of fact there is. I need to borrow a dollar."

Cale was digging into his pocket as soon as the words were spoken. "No problem, I—oops. No money in these pants. Here, I'll get something from the collection plate and put it back later. Come on." He led the way back up the aisle. "We better hurry or we'll miss the dinners."

"As a matter of fact, that's what I want the dollar for. I need to buy lunch."

Bernard stopped. "My goodness, Harrison, if that's all you need, I can certainly provide you with something to eat."

Harrison smiled and ducked his head. He thought he could feel himself begin to blush. "Well actually, it isn't for me alone. I, uh, intend to take a young lady. For a drive and a picnic, you see."

Cale clapped him on the shoulder and grinned. "That is just fine, Harrison. Good for you. And I'm so glad you aren't distressed." He chuckled and began walking back up the aisle toward the stacked collection plates. "And I thought springtime was supposed to be the time for romance. It seems summer will do quite nicely."

"Nicely, indeed," Harrison agreed happily. "But why-ever should I be distressed about anything?"

"Oh, my own meddling nature, I suppose. I'm a frus-trated matchmaker at heart, really. I had gotten the impression you were sweet on the Trope girl, that's all."

Harrison stopped, and it took Bernard a moment to realize he was walking alone. He stopped and turned back to look. "Did I say something wrong, Harrison?"

"I don't know," Harrison said truthfully. He was confused. "What did you mean about Martha Trope?"

Bernard brightened. "Grand news. Marriages and chris-tenings are two of a preacher's most joyous functions, you know."

"Marriages! But what could that have to do with Martha?"

Cale was still smiling. "Mr. and Mrs. Trope had a word with me before services this morning. They have consented to the betrothal of their daughter to Jesse Howard. They asked me to perform the ceremony." He added quickly, "After, of course, an appropriate period. I told them it would be a—Harrison? Harrison! Where are you going? Did I say something—?"

CHAPTER 31

Harrison stumbled blindly out of the church. He lurched down the few steps and nearly fell. Anger welled up behind his eyes and turned them hot. His eyes and his cheeks were wet, and he did not care.

He ran toward his wagon with a staggering gait, as little in control of his balance now as he had been the night he got drunk with Conrad Burton.

He blinked rapidly but could barely see. Head down and tears running, he found the painted spokes he was looking for and flung himself into the driving box. He grabbed up the lines and realized too late that there was a yellow horse between the poles before him, and he had been driving a sorrel. On top of all the other humiliations, he had climbed into the wrong wagon.

"What the hell are you doing?" someone shouted. He could hear quick footsteps as someone ran toward him.

Harrison wiped a hasty sleeve across his eyes and turned.

It was that damned Jesse Howard coming toward him. Of all people, of all the wagons parked near the church, he had chosen to climb into Howard's wagon by mistake.

He looked at the tall, solidly built cowboy and an image came to mind of Jesse Howard with Martha in his arms. A shrill, keening sound began to rise unbidden in Harrison's throat. Before he realized his own intentions, Harrison had launched himself off the driving box straight at Jesse's arrogantly handsome face.

Harrison was no fighter, but his rage blinded him to all thoughts of caution or restraint. He lashed out viciously if without skill, his desire only to hurt or to maim.

121

Jesse, taken completely by surprise, as a man would be if he saw a rabbit attack a hound, did not even raise a hand to defend himself.

Harrison crashed into him, flinging himself through the air from the height of the wagon, and both men fell to the ground with Harrison windmilling wild punches even as they tumbled into the dirt.

By some instinct or forgotten childhood lesson Harrison bounced upright above the sprawling Jesse and kicked out with his foot. The toe of his shoe caught Jesse in the crotch, and the much bigger cowboy blanched and doubled up with pain.

"You son of a bitch, you son of a bitch yousonofabitch," Harrison was screaming over and over with all the shrill power of his quaking voice.

The commotion attracted immediate attention, and men and boys began to run toward them from the other wagons, where families had been unpacking their picnic baskets. Women turned away, and several grabbed their children and tried to hustle them out of sight.

Harrison continued to kick the fallen and now agonized Jesse Howard. He was scarcely aware that he was doing so. The fight had only begun, yet he was breathing as heavily as if he had just run all the way from the Running W. His face was a twisted, blood-engorged mask of raw hate.

A blow, unseen, smashed into the side of Harrison's head, and he went to his knees. He threw himself forward with his hands, curled like talons, clawing for Jesse's throat.

The stitched leather of a boot crashed into Harrison's face, lifting him a foot or more into the air and throwing him onto his back. His face felt suddenly numb and hotly wet at the same time.

He was dimly aware of a face far above his. It was the same damned Texas cow thief called Tom who had been in the saloon that night.

Harrison ignored him and tried to scramble back to the white-faced, doubled-over Jesse, who was still writhing in agony from the unexpected kick.

"You little shit," the Texan snarled. The toe of his

boot slammed into Harrison's ribs. "Sucker a man."
The boot landed again with a force that Harrison could
feel deep in the core of his body. "Kick him when he's
down." The boot sank deep into Harrison's belly with
the force of the kick, and Harrison could hear but not
feel the rush of air from his lungs. "Little shit!" Tom
kicked him again.

Harrison would have told them. He would have told
all of them the dire things he was going to do to them.
But he had no breath left in his body, and the pain was a
consuming fire that left no room for thought or word. It
left no room for anything but hate.

He tried yet again to claw his way to Jesse's de-
fenseless body, but again the Texan's boot crashed into
his head.

This time Harrison did not even feel it.

This time there was only oblivion.

He was unconscious when Jesse Howard was picked
up and carried away by his friends and by the Tropes,
and when Bernard Cale picked up the unconscious form
that would have been left in the dirt outside the church
and carried Harrison away to tend to him.

CHAPTER 32

Harrison was far from alone when he came to more than an hour later. Bernard Cale, Luther MacRae and a number of other men from the town were gathered around him. Harrison blinked and even that small amount of movement hurt. His face ached worst of all, and out of the corners of his eyes he could see some sticking plaster jutting up around his nose. From the way it felt, his nose had not only been broken, it was swollen to several times its normal size.

"You better have a good explanation, boy," the Redbluff constable said sternly when he saw Harrison's eyes open, "or you're going to face charges for assault and maybe some other things when I figure out what they might be."

"I do." Even to himself those brief syllables sounded more like croaking than like words. He struggled but was unable to sit up by himself. After a moment's hesitation, which Harrison did not fail to see, Bernard came forward to ease him into a sitting position and prop a brace of pillows behind his back.

"You'd best say it then, boy." MacRae was hard-faced and serious. For the first time Harrison realized the seriousness of what he had done.

"I couldn't . . . couldn't take any more of it," Harrison said slowly. He was speaking slowly and with precision to give himself time to organize his thoughts as he went along. The men would certainly accept his slowness of speech as a result of his injuries, although in truth his throat and tongue were among the very few parts of his body that did not hurt at the moment.

He paused and as he expected they waited for him to continue at his own pace.

"Bernard . . . Bernard told me. About Jesse marrying Martha. She, Martha Trope that is, is a fine girl. Too good a girl for the type of person Jesse Howard has shown himself to be."

"What the hell business of yours is that, boy?" the constable demanded.

"None," Harrison said slowly, "except that she is a friend." Well, that was the simple truth. More or less. Any ideas he might have had in excess of that statement were his own. And they were quite thoroughly dissipated now. Harrison shoved that knowledge into a far recess of his mind. It would not do to examine it now.

"So?"

"So—" He halted.

Harrison looked at Luther MacRae's stony face and at the hard, set expressions of the other men as well. Even Bernard was looking at him with cold suspicion. The prospect of criminal charges, perhaps even a jail term, was all too near.

"So I could take no more," Harrison said calmly. "I have been living in fear of those men for too long already. When I heard that one of that stripe was going to marry such a fine, decent, genuinely good person as Miss Trope, well, I just could not remain quiet any longer."

Harrison hung his head and turned his eyes away from the men. "I know I should have told you about this a long time ago, Mr. MacRae. It is to my shame that I did not."

"Told me what, boy?"

"Those men. Those Texans. And Jesse too, I believe."

"Yes?"

"They are the men who have been stealing cattle hereabouts." He was not looking at them, but Harrison could well imagine the widening eyes his statement was causing, the expressions of disbelief and probably of quick anger too. "And I believe they may have killed Uncle Stewart also. I am sure they would have killed me if they had discovered me spying on them that day."

Harrison closed his eyes and sank back into the pillows Bernard had plumped for him.

CHAPTER 33

Harrison genuinely did not expect the reaction that his statement caused. Among the men who had come along with Redbluff's part-time constable was Jace Creighton, a leathery old man given to gloom and long silences. He had been one of the first to take up land on the open range in the area. Harrison had at least a grudging respect for Creighton, if only because the man virtually never talked about the way things had been in the "old times."

Now Harrison saw another side to Creighton.

The old man stepped forward and took Harrison by the shirtfront, ignoring the pain it caused when he shook Harrison's eyes wide open and staring. "You sure about that, boy? You for damn *sure?*"

"Some of it I saw with my own eyes, Mr. Creighton. I saw those Texans driving beef off the Running W down on the south end of the place while Uncle Stewart was hunting for them to the north."

Creighton clamped a work-hardened hand over Harrison's mouth. The experience was not a particularly pleasant one. "Don't say another word, boy. Not just yet. You hold this in for another few hours, eh?" He turned and snapped orders to the other men who were in the room, ignoring Luther MacRae. The men were to immediately gather a group of the older cattlemen and a few of the hired hands. Creighton rattled off the names of the men he wanted. When he turned back to Harrison he said, "Your uncle would be in this crowd if he was here now, boy. Your daddy too for that matter. They was good men, both of them."

126

Harrison shook his head. He did not know what was happening.

"Don't you be worryin' about it, boy. You lie still until the others get here. Then you talk it all out, you hear?"

"Yessir." Harrison still did not understand but under the circumstances it probably would be best if he did not argue.

Luther MacRae, however, seemed upset. Normally a phlegmatic man who took a casual approach to his job but performed it in as fair and honest a way as he could, now he was shaken. "You can't do this, Jace," he protested several times. "Not no more, you can't."

"You gonna do it, Luther?" Creighton snapped back at him. "Hell no, you ain't. An' we won't see a hair of our sherf neither. We've had it good here for a lotta years, Luther. We ain't gonna start the old ways again. No, sir, we ain't."

"That's what I'm trying to tell you, Jace. We don't need the old ways around here. Not *any* of them."

"Some ways I expect we do, Luther." Creighton's tone was stony, and cords of muscle bulged at his jaw as he gritted his teeth.

"I won't have it," MacRae said.

"Fine," Creighton said harshly. "Stay out of it then. All the way out."

The constable looked angry. He opened his mouth to say something, thought better of it and clamped his mouth shut again. He turned and stomped out of the room.

The other men had already gone as well, leaving Harrison alone with Creighton and Bernard Cale. Bernard looked as puzzled as he was, Harrison noticed.

"Lie back, boy," Creighton advised him. "Lie back an' rest. You'll be busy enough later on."

Harrison still did not understand but he did as he was told. At least it seemed he was no longer being looked on as a pariah after his attack on Jesse Howard.

Before nightfall Creighton had his men gathered. There were half a dozen of them in addition to Jace Creighton.

Four of them were cattlemen, and two were hired hands who had been in the country for most of their lives although they had never started places of their own. Harrison had known all of them for virtually all of his life.

"Tell them, boy. Tell them what you told me a while ago," Creighton ordered. His tone made it clear that this was an order, not a request.

Harrison had had ample time by now to think about the accusations he had made. The more he thought about them the more convinced he became that he was correct. The Texans were responsible for the cattle thefts. Jesse Howard was undeniably friendly with them. At Creighton's urging, Harrison repeated his suspicions, this time going into far greater detail about his observation of the men driving cattle off the Running W range and the fear of discovery he had felt.

"I know I should have come forward and said something sooner," he concluded, "but I was afraid of what they would do if they knew."

"You don't have to be scared of them, boy," Creighton said ominously. "We agree you shoulda spoke up sooner, but no harm's been done." He turned to the other men.

They were a hard-looking crowd, Harrison realized. Exactly the sort of men Harrison wanted to live far away from. They were in their middle years or beyond, but every one of them was sun-baked and roughened by the lives they led. They were, Harrison realized uncomfortably, all heavily armed as well.

"You heard him," Creighton said crisply. "How many of you has lost cattle here lately?"

The hard-set faces nodded. "Sure have," Joe Hardy affirmed. "Not many yet, but I've lost some myself. Last time I seen Stewart he said he was hit pretty bad. Said if it kept up he might could be ruined. We could *all* be ruined if a bunch of slick rustlers hit us."

"Exactly," Creighton said. "Give them bastards a foothold and we're all done for. That's as true now as it was before. An' now it looks like Stewart's gone under trying to fight them for us when we should of got together again 'fore now."

"Again?" The preacher had been silent until now. He had been standing quietly off to the side. Now he moved forward until he was facing Jace Creighton.

"That's right, Bernard, again. It's been a long time and it's a thing we don't talk about, but we've all rode together before. Us and Stewart and Harrison's daddy and a bunch more good men who're dead an' buried now. We don't like it, Bernard, but a man's got to protect himself. Got to take care of his own. It looks like we got to do it again."

Cale looked sick. "You are a vigilance committee, aren't you?"

"We are," Jace Creighton said. His eyes were alight with the fire of vengeance.

CHAPTER 34

The wagon trip had been long and cold and uncomfortable. Harrison felt like he had been receiving a beating the whole night long. Now in the chill, gray light of the predawn he was frightened as well as sore.

Jace Creighton's vigilantes had insisted on bringing him with them on their raid on the Texans' headquarters.

"When a man takes up a gun or a rope, boy, he's got to be certain sure," the old man had said, his voice as booming—and as certain—as Harrison had always imagined the voices of the ancient prophets must have been. "We take no justice, boy, without a fair trial beforehand."

Creighton and his men had loaded Harrison onto a wagon over Bernard Cale's protests and his own.

Now the wagon was hidden in a shallow swale not more than a hundred yards from the dugout where the Texans had chosen to make their home. By sitting upright on the bed of folded blankets in the wagon box, Harrison could see the door of the dugout and the scantling corral nearby. There was a curl of smoke coming from the sheet metal chimney at the back of the dugout. There had been no smoke when they first arrived almost an hour earlier.

"All right, boys, you know what to do," Creighton said. "Joe, you got the wadding?"

Hardy nodded.

"Slip in easy then so they won't hear us. The rest of us will be on the sides."

Joe Hardy checked to see that the revolver he was carrying was free in its pouch. He pulled a large handful of rags from his saddlebags. The other men, including

Creighton, took up the rifles and shotguns they had brought along.

Harrison swallowed hard. He wished now that he had not spoken, no matter how right he was about the men. But now his fear of the vigilance group was greater than his fear of the three brothers from Texas and of Jesse Howard.

Hardy took his boots off and set them on the ground beside his horse. He replaced them with a worn pair of moccasins from his other saddlebag pocket. "I'm ready," he whispered.

"Go on then. We'll give you a start."

The men watched while Hardy loped in a circle around the Texans' earthen shelter, toward the back of the place. When he was about even with the dugout they started forward on foot themselves. Harrison watched with a horrified concentration.

All of the men walked softly with their weapons held at the ready. They split into two groups and took up positions to the sides of the single doorway leading into the dugout that was carved from the slope of a rolling hill.

Beyond them Joe Hardy slowed as he neared the sod-covered roof of the dugout. Moving very slowly now, he crept forward with his bundle of rags until he reached the back end of the dugout. Stretching forward, presumably to avoid stepping on the pole and sod roof that had been laid over the dugout, he removed the rain cap from the stovepipe and stuffed the pipe with rags.

Harrison understood finally. Within moments the smoke from the Texans' breakfast fire would fill the dugout. They would almost certainly believe it to be an accidental blockage and would not be alarmed when they came running out to remove the block.

The plan worked so smoothly that Harrison wondered how many other times in the distant past these same men had used the same trick to force men out into the open.

A minute went by but little more. From a distance Harrison could hear nothing of what might have been said inside the dugout, but the door was flung wide and all three Texans came stumbling into the yard in their drawers, rubbing their eyes and looking back toward the roof of their shelter. None of them was armed.

Creighton or one of the others—Harrison guessed it would have been Creighton—apparently said something. The Texans froze into position where they were and looked cautiously around.

The sight that greeted them was a ring of gaping muzzles leveled at their stomachs. They raised their hands, and Joe Hardy came around to join the other men from Redbluff. Hardy had his revolver out and cocked.

Creighton turned and said something to Bert Payton, who was nearest him. Payton came at a dogtrot to the wagon where Harrison was waiting, climbed quickly into the seat and drove the team up to the front of the dugout.

"Are these the men?" Creighton demanded without preamble.

"Yes, sir," Harrison answered in a shaky voice.

"What the *hell* is this all about?" the oldest of the Texans demanded. He was the one called Tom. None of them, Harrison realized, looked particularly dangerous or threatening as they stood in the pale morning light wearing sagging drawers and barefoot. They now looked more confused and frightened than belligerent.

Harrison swallowed. "Those are the men," he said in a firmer voice.

CHAPTER 35

Tom, Chuck and Michael Bayles looked like they had aged twenty years in the few hours since dawn. Jace Creighton's vigilance committee had allowed them to put on boots and trousers but nothing more. They looked haggard. Only Tom looked angry as well. The younger brothers only seemed frightened.

Tom looked up toward the bright glare of the relentless plains sun. It was not yet midmorning but he and his brothers were running sweat under their arms and down their faces. None of the other men were affected by it.

"I've told you a dozen times already, dammit," he said wearily. "Sure this idiot might of seen us with some beeves. We're trying to start a herd here, for cryin' out loud. We brought in some bulls. Bought-and-paid-for bulls. When we get our stock cows bought we'll upgrade our beef with them bulls. Sure we brought them in across the Wilke place. Hell, man, it's open range, ain't it? Nothing wrong with a man driving beeves across open range."

Jace Creighton's jaw had retained its firm set from the beginning. He did not soften now, as he had not during any of the retellings. "I understand all that, Bayles, but I've never yet met a man that wouldn't lie to save his own neck, me included."

"Look, dammit, *write* to the man. He can tell you. We bought them bulls off Horace Walch down in the Indian Nations. They're recalling near all of the grazing leases down there. Opening the land for settlement." Bayles shook his head. "Jesus, I wisht now we'd taken up land down there ourselves. But we didn't. And we bought them bulls. I've shown you the bill of sale, for

Christ's sake. It's only natural that Walch would be running a W brand too. Jesus!"

Creighton heard him out impassively. "It makes no difference," he said when Bayles came to a stop. "Even if you were telling the truth about the bulls, which I damn well doubt in light of the evidence, Harrison being an eyewitness and all, there is still the murder of Stewart Wilke to be answered. I don't suppose you have a bill of sale for that too."

Tom Bayles looked agonized. His brothers merely seemed numb. "I've told you and told you, old man. My brothers and me don't know nothing *about* Mr. Wilke. Far as I can recall none of us has ever laid eyes on the man. Hell, you yourselves say *you* don't know anything except that he's missing. Nobody's found a body. Maybe nobody ever will. We all know a man can come up missing in country this big an' no one ever know the truth about where he's gone or what's happened to him. His horse could of throwed him. He could of got after whoever really is stealing stock around here and they might of shot him. Lord, man, just because this Wilke fella is missing is no reason to think we had anything to do with it."

"Stewart was chasing the cattle thieves," Creighton said patiently. "We have a witness who can testify that you three are those cattle thieves. With Stewart missing it is a fair assumption that the men he was chasing had something to do with his disappearance. No, Bayles, it is our firm conviction that you are responsible for the disappearance and probable death of Stewart Wilke. And however you might handle things in Texas, in Kansas we will not abide lawlessness."

"My God, man, this here is lawlessness," Bayles cried.

"This," Creighton said, "is justice. Where there cannot be law there can at least be justice. It is our responsibility to insure it."

"Then put us in jail. Put us in jail until you can write to Horace Walch. He'll tell you about them bulls."

"And the other missing cattle? Will he tell us about them too?"

"We don't know anything about any missing cattle. Believe me, we don't have so many that we wouldn't notice if any of ours was gone. We don't know anything about missing cows."

Creighton gave him a tight-lipped smile. "An interesting point, isn't it? Each of us has lost a few head. Stewart lost a great many. Yet you three say you have not lost a single beef. Coincidence, Bayles? Or more evidence of your guilt. The latter, I would have to believe."

Tom Bayles looked at his brothers. "I don't know any other way to put it."

Chuck, who appeared to be the middle brother, said nothing. He looked away, gazing dumbly off toward the horizon.

Michael did not speak either. He swallowed hard, then seemed to screw up his courage. He gave his brother a wink, worked his mouth for a moment and directed a wad of spit toward Jace Creighton. He missed.

"He's not the son of a bitch you ought to spit at," Tom said. "That stinkin' little nance in the wagon is the lying little bastard that started the lies."

"Calm down," Creighton said. He did not sound at all upset that Michael had spit at him. At the moment he seemed completely immovable, detached from emotions.

Tom glared at him, then started toward Harrison, who was still lying in the wagon bed.

"Stop," Creighton ordered. "We have no desire to cause pain here. But we will rope you down and tie you if that is required."

Tom stopped. He looked at Harrison with loathing. "When we get out of this," he said, his voice shaking with anger, "I hope you're handy, boy. I'll make you think yesterday was a quiet walk by the riverside."

Harrison blinked and turned his eyes away. He was stiff and aching in nearly every part of his body. He was also afraid. If the Bayles brothers did convince the vigilance committee . . .

"No more of that," Creighton said mildly. He sighed.

"I expect the best thing here would be to tie your hands. Will you have it the easy way?"

Tom Bayles gritted his teeth, but after a moment he nodded. "All we want, mister, is a chance to prove our story. You can keep us locked up as long as it takes. We won't try an' make it hard on anybody. We won't fight with you. Hell, that'd just make you all the more sure we're guilty. And we ain't. So we'll go along with you. Tied like a bunch of damn hogs if that's what it takes to make you see we ain't lying. Just put us in the damn jail an' write to Horace Walch. He'll set this straight in no time."

"They won't tie me," Michael said.

"They will," Tom told him. "And not a one of us is gonna lift a finger to keep them from it. You hear me, Mike? We let them take us in. We don't give them no excuses to act anything but fair. Hear me, Mike? Chuck?"

Chuck nodded. Michael took longer to reach his decision, but eventually he too agreed.

One of the men produced a handful of piggin' strings, and the Texans allowed themselves to be bound.

"All right," Creighton said. He sounded tired now and for the first time seemed reluctant to go on. "I'm sorry, boys, but we just can't have cow stealing here. None of us is in good enough shape to stand it."

"Hell, we understand that," Bayles said. "We couldn't neither if we were the ones losing animals."

"All right then. But you might not know," Creighton said, "that we have a sheriff who doesn't much care about Redbluff, and there's a bunch of bleeding hearts in town these days. If we was to carry you back to town there'd just be a lot of talk and nothing ever would get done. Sooner or later some smart son of a bitch would decide that you ought to have a lawyer or that you just ought to be turned back loose to go on stealing cows." He sighed. "We just can't have that."

Bayles went pale. "You can't—" He began to struggle, trying to get his hands free, but each of the brothers was flanked now by a vigilance committee member.

"Justice is necessary," Creighton said.

"You can't—!"

"We have no choice. Joe?"

Hardy nodded.

"I don't know of a tree within a mile of here. Unhitch the team, would you please?"

Hardy nodded and began unhooking the traces of the wagon that had brought Harrison to the dugout. He led the team away from the wagon and tied them to the rails of the Bayles corral. Another of the men took one of the Bayleses' own ropes and ran it through the eye of the tip end of the wagon tongue.

Harrison watched with growing understanding. There were no trees suitable for a hanging within miles. But the upended wagon tongue would be more than high enough to suspend a man off the ground. Tilted back, it should rise ten feet or so. Harrison thought about the one hanging he had seen before and began to gag.

He wanted to stop it. He doubted that he could. Worse, if he did— The thought of what the Texans would do to him. The thought about what Jace Creighton's old-time vigilance committee might also do to him. They were too much to think about.

Besides, he was right. The Bayles brothers had been the ones who were doing the stealing. He had seen them himself.

At least this time no one would force him to watch. At least this time he could close his eyes to the sight and close his ears to the sounds they would make when they hanged. Harrison felt sick.

"Jace," one of the men said.

"Mmmm?"

"Someone's coming."

Harrison and all of the others looked. Across the grass, at least a half hour's ride distant, they could see a horseman coming at a hard run.

"Do you think we should hurry this up?" the man asked.

"No," Creighton said firmly. "We have never yet done anything that we would be ashamed of. If there is something we should know, we will wait to hear it.''

Harrison was glad he had not had any breakfast. He was sure if he had anything in his stomach it would come up now.

CHAPTER 36

Harrison breathed easier. The man on the lathered horse was Jesse Howard. Harrison recognized him well before he reached the Bayles dugout. How he could stand to be racing across the county on horseback after the painful injury he had received not twenty-four hours earlier was something Harrison could not imagine, but it was certainly Jesse on the bay horse.

The sight of him brought back sharp, ugly memories of the way Martha had played with Harrison's affections while choosing to give herself to a brainless cowboy who smelled of sweat and dung. Harrison shoved all of that from his mind.

"He's one of them, I think," he said quickly. "At least Howard is damn sure friendly with this crowd. Don't trust anything *he* might have to say."

"Believe me, I won't," Jace Creighton said. His expression had become even harder, and his voice was tight.

Jesse was stepping out of his saddle even before he had his horse hauled down from its run. The rope-trained animal sat down over its hocks and slid to a stop as Howard leaped to the ground and ran to join them. It was the horse that had been doing all the work of the long run from Redbluff to the Bayles camp, but Jesse was breathing heavily.

"Damn you, Creighton, and *you*—!" Without warning he jumped at Harrison's throat, and it took several of the vigilantes to stop and hold him.

"Thank God you've come," Tom Bayles said. The men ignored him.

"Damn you, Jace Creighton. You and this whole murdering crowd. You haven't learned a damn thing in all these years, have you?"

Creighton colored, but he stood his ground.

"You're just like your father, Howard."

"I'll stand damn proud if that's the truth. Let these boys go, Creighton. This miserable little weasel here is the only one that's done anything wrong. Until now, that is. You and the rest of these men are about to make it worse."

"Shut up, boy, or I'll have you whipped the same as I did your father."

"The way I heard it," Jesse said, "it took the whole cowardly bunch of you to thrash him. I expect it will take you all to put me down too."

Harrison was not sure what they were talking about, but there was no question that there was bitterness between them.

"Listen to me," Jesse insisted, "the whole thing is Harrison's fault. You can't listen to a little liar like he is, for Pete's sake. You can't hang three good men on the word of a mealy-mouthed tweedledee who's pissed off because he got jilted. For God's sweet sake, Creighton, for once in your life listen to reason. You can't let the same thing happen here that happened before."

Creighton had been coldly impassive until now. Now he flushed dark red. "You shut your mouth, Jesse Howard, or show me some proof. We were right before, and we are dead right now. We *will* have justice in this country."

The two men, one old and craggy, the other young and strong, stood nose to nose and glared at each other.

Harrison touched the elbow of Joe Hardy, who was standing near him. "What's this all about, Mr. Hardy?"

Hardy sniffed. "I'd of thought you'd have heard all about it."

Harrison shook his head.

"Back when you were a little bitty thing. An' that Jesse too for that matter. His daddy tried to stop the committee from hanging a horse thief. The son of a bitch tried to say he'd found the horse and was bringing it in when he was caught red-handed with a Running W horse at the end of his lead rope. Caught him cold, they did. Jace an' Stewart an' your daddy hanged the son of a bitch. Just as they ought to've done. Howard tried to stop them.''

It had always been understood that the Wilkes and the Howards did not like each other. No one had ever told Harrison why that was so.

Not that it was a matter of great interest. Not at this point. As a matter of fact, the renewal of the dispute now, after all the years that must have passed, would only serve to help discredit Jesse Howard. Harrison withheld the smile that tried to creep onto his face. All in all, he thought, this was working out better than he could have hoped.

Creighton turned to Harrison. ''Was this . . . *person* here,'' he said it with obvious distaste, ''with them when they were stealing your uncle's cattle?''

Harrison stared at Jesse. It was tempting. A word or two . . . No, he thought. Jesse might well have an alibi for where he had been that day. The risk was not worth the gamble. ''No, sir,'' he said, ''just the three of them.'' He pointed accusingly toward the bound Bayles brothers.

''What are you talking about?'' Jesse demanded. ''What day? What damned cattle? Hell, I'll vouch for these boys. I'll—''

''You'll shut your mouth is what you'll do. We all know you'd lie to keep us from doing our duty. You are no better than the man who sired you. I'd thought there was hope for you, boy. Thought all of this was forgotten. But I see that isn't so. Well, so be it. But do *not* presume to interfere with the business of your betters.''

''Dammit, Creighton, if you won't take my word on it that these are good, honest boys from Texas, then get some proof, will you? I know you don't have any. You can't. These boys aren't guilty of anything.''

''Harrison Wilke saw them, Jesse. He saw them with his own eyes, driving cattle off the Wilke range. Ask him yourself if you don't believe me.''

''What he saw was us bringing in those—'' Tom Bayles started to say. He was brought to a rude halt with a grunt of pain when one of the men jabbed a shotgun butt into his stomach. "Shut up and speak when you're spoken to," the vigilante growled.

Even Creighton was so angry now, after Jesse Howard's arrival, that he made no protest about mistreatment of the men who were about to be hanged. Until then he had made it a point to remain soft-spoken and aloof.

Jesse looked Harrison in the eyes, and several of the men poised, ready to grab him if he made another leap toward the injured Harrison.

"I saw them," Harrison said coldly. He was feeling better and better. Soon the Texans would be out of the way. He would not have to be afraid of them any longer. And Jesse, when this was done Martha Trope's high-handed suitor would be discredited before all the community. With any luck at all, Mrs. Trope would refuse her consent to a wedding with Jesse, and Martha could return to the side of a person who was worthy of her affections.

"Dammit—" Jesse began.

"Shut up, boy. We'll hear no more of it," Creighton warned. "Try to oppose us, and we will truss you up the same as they are."

"If you won't listen to me, dammit, listen to someone you will believe. They know in town what's going on out here, you know."

"We are doing only what is right," Creighton said.

"You're doing what—ah, why should I try to explain anything to your kind? Look, I know you're proud of your bunch of murderers. The whole town knows you are. They even know it used to be the only way to get anything done around here. But that's a long time ago. Even Mr. Holton and Mr. Yates oppose you now. At least as far as these boys are concerned." He motioned toward the tied and uncomfortable Bayles brothers. "They heard you'd come out here, and when I left town they were hitching a buggy to come out themselves. At least wait and see what they have to say before you do anything that can't be undone. Is that too much to ask?"

Creighton gave him a sharp look. "Charles is driving out here? And Yates?"

"Yes. Maybe more. I know they're coming."

"Yates is a damn lawyer," Joe Hardy said. "He'll go to spouting writs and rights, Jace. I wouldn't trust him."

"Yates has been along on a night ride or two himself," Creighton said. "I just don't know."

"Listen," Jesse pleaded, "I know there's still some doubt about what happened the last time. Maybe you were even right that time. We'll never know for sure. But dammit, Creighton, this time you can be *sure*. Just *listen* to them. You have your guns and your ropes and your damn wagon tongue. If what they say doesn't make any sense to you, you can still hang these poor boys. There won't be any harm done. And I promise you, I swear to you, Creighton, you won't hear another word of complaint about it out of me or out of my dad. We won't say a thing, an' I won't do a thing to try an' stop you. If it comes to that, I'll help you keep Mr. Holton and Mr. Yates from interfering. Just wait and listen to them. Please."

Creighton folded his arms and stood for a moment deep in thought. At length he nodded. "That is reasonable," he said. "We can wait until they get here. Boys, you might as well take time to fix some dinner. It will take them a while to get a buggy out here. And mind you don't take anything out of that dugout. We did not come here to steal, only to see justice done."

The men scattered to the task, and Jesse led the three Texans to a seat against the dry-laid rock wall that formed the face of their earthen dugout.

Harrison wanted to protest the change in plan. If they were going to do this, they should get it over with. But he said nothing. His stomach was beginning to churn with an anxiety that had nothing to do with hunger. He doubted he would be able to eat anything when the meal was ready.

CHAPTER 37

The buggy arrived just before noon. And Harrison's world caved in.

"Howdy, Jace."

" 'Lo, Charles, Tom." The weathered old rancher waited while the well-dressed townsmen climbed down from the rig, stretched and slapped at the dust that liberally coated their suits. Neither Holton nor Yates seemed particularly upset. They nodded pleasantly and shook hands all around.

"What can we do for you fellas?" Creighton asked when the amenities were out of the way.

"You can give us a minute of your time," Holton said.

"Anytime, Charles. I expect you know that."

Holton smiled thinly. There would be very few men anywhere in this part of the country who would not be willing to listen when their banker wanted to talk. "I'm glad we got here when we did, Jace," he observed.

"Why is that, Charles?"

"A man doesn't like to see mistakes being made. Especially serious ones."

"And you think we were going to make one?"

"If you were going to hang these boys you sure were."

"I don't know that I can agree with you, Charles. Harrison here saw them himself with—"

"Harrison Wilke wouldn't know his own butt in the morning if he couldn't examine it with both hands," Holton interrupted. He shot a glance toward Harrison that was anything but apologetic.

Harrison quailed before the coldness in the banker's

eyes. His head hurt worse than ever, and he was doubly glad that he had not eaten when the others did.

Creighton's vigilance men were crowding closer. It was obvious from Holton's tone of voice that there was no uncertainty in him.

"These boys came up from Texas to establish here," Holton said, "just the way they've told everyone."

"You can listen to them talk and know they're from Texas," Creighton said.

"That may be so, but this trio didn't come here cold. They came in a while ago and said I could expect a transfer draft from their daddy down in Texas. It came in this morning's mail, just like they said it would."

Creighton shook his head. "That still doesn't prove anything, Charles. Even if the amount is substantial, having money's never been a cure for greed."

"You're right about that," Holton said with a smile, "but that isn't the only thing that came in the morning mail."

Creighton and the others waited for him to go on. The banker seemed to be enjoying himself. He kept looking at Jace Creighton. And at Harrison. "I also got this."

He reached inside his coat and pulled out a soiled, much-traveled brown envelope. It had already been opened.

"I received this letter from Stewart Wilke," Holton said.

Harrison could feel a lump in his throat, and his head began to pound with sharp, vicious bursts of pain each time his heart sent a new burst of blood pumping through his arteries.

"The letter is dated five days ago. He mailed it from Ogllala, Nebraska."

"That certainly proves that the Bayles boys didn't murder Stewart then," Creighton agreed. "They've been close around here for a while now. But it doesn't say a thing to the point of them stealing our cows."

"As a matter of fact it does, Jace. You see, that's the whole point of the letter. It seems Stewart had himself one hell of a chase after those thieves. You know he's a stubborn old son of a bitch, though. He won't quit a chore once he's taken it on. He didn't quit this one either.

"According to what Stewart writes here," he said, moving his head so he was addressing all of the men and not only Creighton, "Stewart was still working it out when his hands caught up with him. They followed the cow thieves all the way north into Nebraska and caught up with them at the Ogllala shipping pens.

"Seems those boys had registered the Running W brand up there in Nebraska and had been selling Running W beef there for the past few months. Stewart and his boys had a discussion with them. That is the way he put it, in any event. A discussion. Stewart came away from it with a bullet in his leg, which is why he has not returned yet. The thieves came out somewhat the worse.

"Fortunately two of them—there had been four to begin with—were in a condition to talk. They were also in a mood for conversation. Stewart does not explain his methods of persuasion."

Creighton grinned. "Doubt that he needs to, actually. A man kind of knows it when old Stewart gets mad."

"Exactly," Holton agreed. "Among the things the cattle thieves mentioned was that they were recruited and brought in here for the specific purpose of bleeding the Running W range of its salable beef. Apparently they also picked up a little extra money by running off other cattle as well, but their primary purpose in being here, after being assured the pickings would be remarkably easy after so long without trouble in this country, was to ruin the Running W.

"In spite of the size of his holdings and the number of his cattle, Stewart has been in little better financial position than any of you men. And you all know how poor the cattle market has been the past few years."

That brought a nod of agreement from each of the men except Harrison, who neither knew nor cared anything about the market for livestock, and Jesse Howard, who seemed to be thinking about other things. Jesse was already busy untying the hands of the Bayles brothers. Even Chuck was nodding his agreement with the plight of the stockman.

"The Wilke property would not have lasted long. And Stewart's talkative thieves say there would have been other properties targeted for large-scale thefts in the future. As soon as the Running W had gone under. Apparently their intention was to register legal brands in adjoining states or territories for the target herds, drive the cattle long distances but then be able to market them apparently within the law."

"Damn," someone muttered.

"You said these men were recruited?" Jesse asked. He joined the group with the Texans at his side, rubbing their wrists now and looking worse for wear but much relieved.

"I did," Holton said. "By a very ambitious young man too. I almost admire his industry if not his methods."

Jesse immediately turned to send an accusing glance toward Harrison.

The banker laughed. "Don't be foolish, Jesse. Despite his high opinion of himself, Harrison hasn't the brains to think of something like this."

"Come to think of it, Mr. Holton, I guess you're right at that."

"No, the young man with the large greed is my now former clerk Conrad Burton."

Harrison felt the blood rush from his head, and he became suddenly cold. This was not possible. None of it.

"The thieves were happy enough to tell Stewart everything they knew about the whole scheme. Conrad recruited them with extravagant promises, which they admit were being met. However, when it came to a question of going to jail alone or in company they decided he should have some of that reward also. They say Conrad even had some scheme—they were not sure about the details except to know that there was something planned—to leech the cash flow away from the Running W and make Conrad's takeover easier." Holton shrugged. "I don't know anything about that. Not yet, anyway. Stewart does little banking with us, but I know he has made no major withdrawals lately."

Harrison began to shake. Oh Lord, he thought miserably. Charles Holton might not know what that plan had been. Harrison did know. He lay down in the bed of the wagon and curled himself into a tight ball with his eyes squeezed shut. He began to rock back and forth with small, regular movements.

"Where's young Burton now?" Creighton asked.

"Luther MacRae paid him a visit shortly after the mail arrived this morning," Holton said. "He's waiting for us back in Redbluff. We don't have to hurry. Conrad will be there whenever we get back to town."

There was a silence for a time. Then finally Creighton spoke again. "Bayles, I . . ." He could not go on. He sounded very old.

There was a long pause. Apparently even Jesse did not want to remind the man of what he had almost done.

Tom Bayles said, "We're going to be neighbors here for a long time, old man. But I hope you don't ever get it in mind that we'll ever be friends."

"I—no, I won't expect that."

The men turned away and began to drift silently toward their horses. Harrison felt the wagon shift and tilt as someone, he did not even look to see who it was, climbed onto the seat. He heard someone else walk the team into place and hitch them. Within minutes the men were on their way back to Redbluff.

CHAPTER 38

The teamster shifted his wad to the other cheek, took aim and sent a stream of brown tobacco juice into the dust near the hooves of his near-wheeler. He took a fresh hold on his lines and turned to look at the passenger he had picked up several miles back.

"You all right, boy?"

The passenger nodded.

"Sure look down in the mouth," the freighter observed. "Not that it's any of my business, but it's kinda curious finding a man way the hell out here in the middle of nothing and him afoot. Real curious, for a fact."

The passenger did not answer.

"Your business, of course," the freighter said cheerfully. He seemed to be used to being alone and gave the impression that if there was no human available to talk to he would be as happy talking to his horses.

"A fella on the drift, though, I expect he's likely to wind up anywhere. Now me, I don't mind bein' out in the middle of the big grass country. Nope, don't mind that at all. Kinda restful, in fact. And when you do run into folks around here, why, you'll find that they're the salt of the earth, son. I'm telling you, and it's a fact. They're fine people around here. Honest and decent is what they are. It's a hard land an' sometimes a visitor, 'specially an eastern fella—'scuse me but I'd guess that that's what you are, judgin' from the way you're dressed—a person that don't know the country, he might think the people are hard too. They ain't, though. They're square as square can be, and I don't mean just to a Brother who's done the traveling. If you know what I mean."

149

He looked sideways toward his passenger and shook his head. "No, I guess you don't know what I mean there. Skip it. Anyway, what I was saying, out here in the middle of nothing but grass you'll find some awful good folks. You be straight with them an' they'll be absolutely straight with you, right down the line." He shifted his chew and spat again, this time aiming near the off-wheeler.

"Give 'em time and get to know them, why, I'll bet you'll learn the same. Of course I'd guess that you're new here. But you'll learn. An' all you got to remember is to be straight with them. That's all they'll ever ask of you. Nothing more'n that. You hungry?" He reached into a sack by his feet and pulled out a cold biscuit. "Got more of these here. You're welcome to them." He took a bite. His passenger bent down and took out a handful of the day-old biscuits. He ate with hunger, the teamster saw. But he still said nothing.

"Those biscuits now, my old lady made them up for me before I left home. She always makes up a big poke of them for me to carry along because she knows I like her cooking better'n anyone's. A man eats good enough along the road, but it ain't the same as the cooking at home." He grinned, and a thin trickle of brown juice escaped from the side of his mouth, disappearing quickly into his beard.

"Far as I'm concerned," he said, "that's one of the best reasons a man could have for getting married. There's lots of fellows who disagree, and of course they're entitled to that. But I figure a good woman waiting at the end of the run with a pan of bakin' powder biscuits and a soft bed, why, that's about as good as a man can expect in life."

They drove on for a while in silence. "Have some more," he said when the passenger's biscuits were gone. "She always packs up more than I could possibly get around before they go stale. Dry country like this, things do go stale pretty quick. That's something you have to get used to, but that's nothing. You get used to it. And pretty soon you learn to really love it out here. The country an' the people too. You'll learn. You got a girl back home, son?''

"No." The passenger stood in the driving box, moving slowly and with care as if he were an invalid. He climbed over the back of the seat and burrowed into a gap in the lashed and tarp-covered load and closed his eyes to sleep.

The teamster shrugged and turned his eyes back to the dry, dusty road that stretched out ahead for all the miles between Kansas and the Rocky Mountains. "You'll learn," he mumbled, more to himself than to the passenger.

About the Author

Frank Roderus is a former newspaper reporter. He lives in Florissant, Colorado, where he raises quarterhorses and continues his research of the American West.

Among his previous novels are: THE ORDEAL OF HOGUE BYNELL; COWBOY; OLD KYLE'S BOY; JASON EVERS, HIS OWN STORY; SHEEPHERDING MAN; and HELL CREEK CABIN.

LEAVING KANSAS received the Western Writers of America Spur Award for the Best Western Novel of 1983. The trilogy of Harrison Wilke will continue in the forthcoming novels REACHING COLORADO and FINDING NEVADA.